"COME INTO MY PARLOR . . ."

Dolores Aguillar walked toward Ruff Justice, hips moving gently from side to side, her unpinned hair tumbling down across her shoulders. Her fingers were at the nape of her neck, undoing the snap so that her dress could fall to the floor.

"Lie down on my bed, Ruff Justice, and take your clothes off," she said. It was a royal command.

She was beautiful, but oh so cold, a black widow, a preying thing, dark eyes sparkling, lush body provocatively posed. Once she was finished with him she would devour him, Ruff thought.

"I'll make love to you like you've never had it before," she breathed. "I am hungry for you, Justice, do you understand?"

Ruff understood. . . .

Wild Westerns by Warren T. Longtree

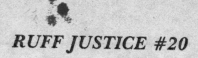

RUFF JUSTICE #20

THE SONORA BADMAN

by
Warren T. Longtree

A SIGNET BOOK

NEW AMERICAN LIBRARY

PUBLISHER'S NOTE

This novel is a work of fiction. Names, characters, places, and
incidents either are the product of the author's imagination or are
used fictitiously, and any resemblance to actual persons, living or
dead, events, or locales is entirely coincidental.

NAL BOOKS ARE AVAILABLE AT QUANTITY DISCOUNTS WHEN
USED TO PROMOTE PRODUCTS OR SERVICES. FOR INFORMA-
TION PLEASE WRITE TO PREMIUM MARKETING DIVISION, NEW
AMERICAN LIBRARY, 1633 BROADWAY, NEW YORK, NEW YORK
10019.

The first chapter of this book appeared in *Frenchman's Pass*, the
nineteenth volume of this series.

SIGNET TRADEMARK REG. U.S. PAT. OFF. AND FOREIGN COUNTRIES
REGISTERED TRADEMARK—MARCA REGISTRADA
HECHO EN CHICAGO, U.S.A.

SIGNET, SIGNET CLASSIC, MENTOR, PLUME, MERIDIAN and NAL BOOKS
are published by New American Library,
1633 Broadway, New York, New York 10019

First Printing, June, 1985

1 2 3 4 5 6 7 8 9

PRINTED IN THE UNITED STATES OF AMERICA

RUFF JUSTICE

He knew the West better than any man alive—a hostile, savage land rife with both violent outlaws and courageous adventurers. But Ruff Justice had a sixth sense that kept him breathing and saw his enemies dead. A scout for the U.S. Cavalry, he was paid to protect the public, and nobody was faster at sniffing out a killer, a crook, a con man—red or white, at close range or far. Anyone on the wrong side of the law would have to reckon with the menace of Ruff's murderously sharp stag-handled bowie knife, with his Colt pistol, and the Spencer rifle he cradled in his arms.

Ruff Justice, gentleman and frontier philosopher— good men respected him, bad men feared him, and women, good and bad, wanted him with all the wildness of the Old West.

1

Fort Bowie, Arizona Territory

The sun went down with a flourish and the dogs of the tiny Spanish town yapped in appreciation. The long-legged woman with the bright, sensuous smile came out of the adobe house and turned for Ruff Justice, who took it all in. She wore a striped skirt and a white blouse that came down off the shoulders, revealing smooth coffee-colored skin. Her hips were full, rounded, and competent. Her breasts jutted against the fabric of her blouse, lifting it, making it something more than a few bits of cloth sewn together, bringing it to a life of its own.

Her name was Alicia.

"Do you like it? My new blouse, Ruffin Justice?"

"I do like it," Ruffin Tecumseh Justice allowed. "All of it."

They were standing before the adobe house in the dusty yard as the sundown glow reddened the walls of the tilted buildings up and down the crooked street. Beyond the adobes stood Fort Bowie, dismal, sun-baked, trying to maintain its military dignity, not quite managing it.

"You are ready?" she asked. She stepped into his arms and kissed him, her lips light and searching.

"Always ready," he replied.

"No, naughty man." She put her finger on his lips. "Ready to eat?"

"Yes."

Alicia cocked her head to one side and looked again at the tall man before her. He was supposed to be very strong, very *fuerte*, but with her he was always gentle. He was a scout for the army and had been helping them look for Sandfire, an Apache. Yet now he wore a ruffled shirt, dark trousers and coat, a black hat with a huge brim, a string tie. His hair was long and dark, as smooth and pretty as Alicia's own blue-black hair. He wore a mustache that drooped past his jawline. He was tall, very tall, and very amusing—yet at times he was far away from Alicia, even when they made love, which he did with great enthusiasm and skill.

Now she hooked his arm with her own, and together, her head on his shoulder, they strode up the dusty street toward the cantina. There Alicia's sister, Rosita, sang; there Uncle Fernando served his famous tamales, made from the succulent flesh of kid roasted over coals in an open pit. That, and much salsa, many tortillas and beans. There she and this Ruff Justice danced around the floor to the mariachi band, to the delight of the onlookers. There they laughed together and then went back to Alicia's house, to her bed, to strip off their clothes and join their heated bodies.

It was hot in the street still. It was late spring in Arizona and it was always hot.

"You are going back soon, back north?" Alicia asked.

"You know I am."

"You must?"

"Yes," Ruff Justice answered.

"But you never found this butcher, Sandfire."

"No, and I don't think we ever would find him. When the Hopi scouts gave it up, I knew I was overmatched. He's lost us and likely's in Mexico now, laughing himself silly over the incompetence of the U.S. cavalry and its civilian scout . . . what was his name?"

He looked at Alicia and frowned, and she laughed, and since it was a lovely laugh and since the night was young and they were going to dance and eat and laugh and make love, Ruff Justice stopped in the middle of the street and kissed her.

"*Ai*, hombre, you take my appetite away."

"Fine. Let's turn around, then."

"No. I told Rosita tonight we would be there. She has a new song."

"All right."

"You are not angry?"

"Of course not. Don't pout either. We'll have a time of it tonight."

"And later . . ."

"Of course." He kissed the top of her head and walked her toward the cantina, which was called La Paloma. Twilight was making purple shadows in the alleyways, beneath the awnings of the buildings. A last effort of the dying sun stretched gold lace across the western horizon, where low clouds hung sheer and dry-looking. Everything looked dry in and around Fort Bowie. Everything was. Water was a precious commodity. It wasn't wasted on flowers and shrubs, on livestock. Some of the people didn't believe in wasting it on washing.

Nothing grew out in the wasteland beyond the town. Between Bowie and the Peloncillo Mountains to the east there was only rocky desert stroked here and there with the dull green of yucca or the gray of smoke trees. There was thorny mesquite in abundance, much cholla cactus, some ocotillo, but only the wild things could find sustenance out there.

It was a land Ruff Justice had spent some time in, but he had never grown to like it despite the sometimes spectacular beauty of it.

He was a northern man, a man of the plains, but the army had wanted him down south to help look for the Chiricahua Sandfire, and so he had come.

"You are silent," Alicia said. It was no new mood for this tall man, but it puzzled her and left her feeling alone when he drifted away like that. The young vaqueros of the town never let their attention drift away from Alicia.

"I was thinking of Sandfire again."

"Wishing you had caught him?"

"Yes. He's the sort you can't feel pity for. I wish they'd caught him and hung him."

"I wish worse for him," Alicia said with some passion. She had lost two cousins to Sandfire's knife. She shook the anger aside. She had promised that she would not worry about anything tonight.

The cantina was brightly lit. Guitar music drifted out into the street. Several army horses were tied up in front, and inside, all was gaiety. No one else was worried about the failure of the army to capture the cutthroat Chiricahua. The soldiers were happy to be back off the desert, to be drinking green beer and raw tequila, to be eating mountains of hot Mexican food and dancing with the señoritas.

Ruff's own mood lifted as soon as he walked in the door. Sgt. Ward, who had been bitten by a sidewinder on the trek, was there looking pale but cheerful, his right hand still swollen. He waved to Ruff.

Alicia's Uncle Fernando came rushing to greet them, a jovial, bearded man with a potbelly and a single gold tooth.

"Almost late! Hello, Ruffin Justice. Your table was hard to hold tonight, Alicia. Shame. What have you been doing? Never mind, don't tell me, I don't want to know." He was leading them across the crowded room now. Heads lifted and men made cracks to Ruff, who smiled back or waved. "Your sister is going on in five minutes. How will you eat now? You'll have to wait until after."

They had arrived at a corner table, small, round, empty. Uncle Fernando continued to chatter on as he held out Alicia's chair for her, shouted something in Spanish to a bartender, and then bustled away.

Alicia laughed. "Such a busy man. He didn't ask what I wanted to drink. Well, he'll remember after a while and bring my favorite wine."

The band struck up a new song and there was time for one more dance before Rosita went on. Ruff rose and started to help Alicia up.

It was then the trouble started across the room.

The cantina door opened and closed as it had been doing constantly, but there was something about the way it happened, the authoritative sound as it slapped closed perhaps, that caused people to stop what they were doing and glance that way, knowing that something violent was about to intrude on their world of merriment.

Ruff felt it too. But when he looked to the door, he

saw only two enlisted men and their officer. All held drawn guns, however, and the officer, a tight-lipped, narrow-eyed lieutenant, wore an armband that read "OD," officer of the day.

Their eyes were fixed on a man across the cantina, a man with wide shoulders, square red-bearded face, receding hair, and a plump Mexican woman on his lap. Behind him the window reflected the man's back and shoulders, and Justice imagined he saw the muscles tense beneath the big man's blue uniform.

The officer walked right up to the table, his men behind him.

"Corporal McCoy, I am placing you under arrest."

"You're what?" The corporal laughed in a way that revealed his lack of fear. There wasn't anything to indicate apprehension in McCoy's manner. He still hugged the señorita, who had stopped giggling and seemed badly to want to leave. McCoy held her to him.

"You heard me well enough. I'm placing you under arrest. Please rise and surrender your sidearm."

Then Dutch McCoy threw back his head and laughed again, but before he had stopped laughing, he moved. He drew his army-issue Schofield revolver and fired point-blank into the lieutenant's face.

The officer wore a mask of blood as he turned briefly toward Justice, arms outstretched as if pleading for help, and dropped to the floor, dead.

McCoy meanwhile had thrown the Mexican woman at the two enlisted men, one of whom fired wildly into the ceiling as McCoy, arm over his face, leapt through the window behind him in a shower of glass.

There was a moment's awed silence, mass immobility, then the soldiers raced for the window, surged

12

toward the door. But it was already dark outside and Dutch McCoy was gone into the desert, leaving his kill behind.

And Ruff Justice had the sudden feeling that he wouldn't be going home as soon as he had thought.

He was right about that. The next day Maj. John Cavendish, Bowie's thoughtful-appearing, small commander, called the scout into his office. It was under ninety inside the headquarters building for a change, but then it was scarcely ten o'clock in the morning. Ruff, wearing buckskin trousers and a white cotton shirt, a belt gun—a long-barreled Colt .44 revolver—a bowie knife, and a tan-colored hat, carrying a sheathed .56 Spencer repeating rifle, entered the office without knocking.

"I want him," Cavendish said.

"You sent out a patrol?"

"He beat them to the border. By now he's in Sonora," the major replied. "I had a good young officer, a Lieutenant Oberlies, in charge of that patrol. He exceeded standing orders and went fifteen miles—at a minimum—into Mexico. He's been reprimanded for that. Had it been me, I would have kept going anyway and the hell with it. I also would have lost some rank. We can't rely on the Mexican authorities to do much. We need a civilian. You."

"I was supposed to head back toward Dakota."

"I'll take care of that. What's the matter, Justice, lost your taste for the desert?"

Ruff smiled. "You could say that."

"Well, I don't blame you a bit." Cavendish spoke quickly, clipping off his words. He toyed with a cigar he never lit. "But I want McCoy. He killed one of my officers. I want him badly."

"What made him do it? What was he supposed to be arrested for?" Justice wanted to know. "It was a violent reaction if it was only a minor infraction."

"McCoy has another name. VanPelt. Under that name he's wanted for murder, arson, and bank robbery in Texas. He enlisted to escape from the law. Many do, you know."

"Yes, sir. So I've heard."

"Well, he was spotted by someone who knew him. A new trooper. He reported McCoy to me yesterday. Since that time another matter has come to light. On questioning McCoy's cronies I discovered that he had plans to hold up the army payroll on the fifth of the month. McCoy and four other troopers. He knew he'd hang if he was arrested. That's what caused him to go to gunplay."

"And now he's gone."

"Temporarily."

"Sir?" Ruff asked, though he knew what the man meant.

"You're going to drop down to Sonora and pick him up for us, aren't you?" Cavendish said mildly. And that was the way he gave his commands.

The northern plains would have to wait for a bit. So would Alicia. Ruff Justice rose and nodded a goodbye. Then he went out onto the plankwalk in front of Fort Bowie's orderly room and stood looking southward, toward Mexico, toward Sonora.

2

The sun was an unwinking white eye in a pale sky, glaring down at its primitive domain. The desert went on forever. Occasionally Ruff Justice lifted his eyes to the blinding whiteness of the day, and then only to glance at the notched peak ahead of him that he was using as a landmark.

He rode a strapping buckskin gelding with a black mane and tail, and as Ruff Justice cleared his throat, the horse pricked its ears apprehensively.

"You're going to hear it anyway," Justice said, and he began to sing.

Everyone knew that redheaded lady
That belle of the ballroom, our three-legged Sadie.
She'd dance, and she'd whirl, and she'd leap, and she'd spin
Till she tangled her legs—but she'd get up again.

Yes, she'd dance every dance would our three-legged Sadie,
That belle of the ballroom, that redheaded lady,
She'd dance, and she'd whirl, and she'd leap, and she'd spin
Till one day she married some Siamese twins

Who perfectly matched that redheaded lady,
That belle of the ballroom, our three-legged
Sadie . . .

The horse could stand no more. It shook its head
violently and nickered loudly, cutting Ruff off.

"There's more," Justice said. "You'll like the next
verse." But even a dumb animal can be tormented
only so much, and feeling mercy, Justice abandoned
the song to the desert.

The notched mountain appeared no nearer than it
had an hour ago. Ruff muttered a curse and removed
his hat to wipe his forehead. Sweeping back his long
dark hair, he planted the hat on his head again.

It was hot and dry. The wind was not a cooling
thing, but a breath of hell that rose now and then to
hurl handfuls of sand in Ruff's face or to dance away
across the desert in whirling dust devils.

The desert was a lonesome, empty place, but it had
seen plenty of activity the last few days. Ruff could
still make out the tracks of the cavalry patrol that
had pursued Dutch McCoy southward, penetrating a
little way into Mexico before the young officer got
nervous and turned his column back.

Likely they wouldn't have caught McCoy anyway,
Justice thought, for a cavalry patrol doesn't move all
that quickly. At least not as quickly as a lone man
riding for his skin.

"Straight as an arrow," Ruff mumbled to himself.

McCoy had led that patrol as straight as an arrow
toward the notched peak, which was El Capitán. It
sounded reasonable until you thought about it. The
land was flat and sure, but the easier course was
down the dry river bottoms, which offered no chal-

lenging stands of cactus, no rocky stretches to deal with. This terrain took a considerable amount of horsemanship to get through. The clumps of nopal cactus could grow shoulder-high to a horse and form impossible mazes, acres in size. The rocks were volcanic glass, capable of ripping a horse's hooves to shreds. No, for out-and-out speed, the river bottom was by far the better choice—clean white sand, nothing to bother the animal or possibly lame it.

But Dutch McCoy chose to beeline it toward El Capitán, which gave Ruff Justice cause to think that the murderer had a specific goal in mind, that he wasn't just running for Mexico, but heading for a certain place.

Except there wasn't anyplace to go. Where Dutch was heading there was nothing but badlands. Mile after mile of twisted canyon, *calderas*, cactus, and lava fields.

"Well, maybe I've got too much imagination," Justice muttered. Maybe McCoy was heading this way because he didn't know any better, riding in a straight line because he had been too panicked to think out his course—except McCoy hadn't struck Ruff Justice as an impulsive man. He was a cool one. He killed cold.

Ruff followed the trail of the patrol over a long plateau, where red and black volcanic stone, pocked and glassy, littered the ground, and where a dozen kinds of cactus flourished and little else tried to grow. Looking to his landmark and then turning slightly in his saddle to look back, Ruff decided he was several miles into Mexico.

Back again. He didn't dislike Mexico, but the Sonoran desert wasn't a place he would choose to live in—or to die. Loaded with sidewinders, gila monsters, scorpions, centipedes, and cactus, it offered little else but its eerie, desolate beauty. Odd and bizarre landforms dotted the land, twisted spires and tilted mesas, broken bluffs, long white *playas*. There had been volcanoes here—the cinder cones, the *calderas*, still stood—and there had been a sea. But the *playa* was now a cracked and lifeless sea bottom. If you dug down, you could find a proliferation of ancient shells. Farther east were the remains of a dead forest, petrified logs forty feet long turned to stone.

There had been much life here. Now there was only death. It was a land fit for only the demon things, the thorny, poisonous offerings of the earth—like Sandfire. Sandfire, who enjoyed himself by carving up flesh and burning people, who slaughtered and charred all in his way, who was as elusive as dawn mist on the desert.

The cavalry had turned back. Ruff found the rise where they had halted, their horses milling, and then turned back, the young officer giving up the pursuit, seeing that they weren't going to catch Dutch McCoy, that they were already well into Mexico.

Ruff sat on his buckskin horse, looking out across the flats at the mountains, vast and incredibly rugged. The notion came to him that he might just as well turn back himself. He wasn't going to find Dutch McCoy now. Likely the renegade had doubled back toward Tucson or Yuma, planning on catching a train east.

But when Justice started on, he headed south. After all, the army had asked him to help and he was still taking their pay, so he would have at it.

McCoy's tracks were harder to trail than those of

the entire cavalry patrol, but Justice found them and followed. McCoy hadn't made much effort to cover his sign, and in places he could have made it more difficult by riding over rocks and through loose sand. But he chose not to. He rode southward . . . straight southward.

The day began to cool and the pale-brown mountains turned to a soft violet. Ruff Justice began to look for a place to camp. Anyplace reasonably smooth would have done for him, but he wanted some kind of forage for the horse, and he found it in a dry wash where wispy mesquite stood in ragged ranks. The buckskin wouldn't like mesquite beans, but they would nourish it. The Apache ate them, ground into a flour called *pinole*. Ruff had survived on them once during a bad stretch when he had walked out of another desert, far away and long ago.

He hobbled the horse, unsaddled, slipped the bit, and rolled out his blankets under a huge, shaggy mesquite, watching the sky go to gold and crimson above the mountains.

There were flames in the sky, as well as a fire burning against the dark earth not far to the south. Ruff had seen it as he dismounted, looked twice, and then shook his head in surprise. Someone else was riding south. Someone reckless or powerful, for they had a fire even though the Apache, Sandfire, was still hunting on the desert.

Ruff slept lightly that night and was up early. The hour before dawn was surprisingly cold, and with numb fingers Justice cinched up and bound his bedroll.

The sun was just cresting the horizon when he started south again, riding easy, his eyes alert. He had company out there, and he didn't much like it. He picked up McCoy's tracks a mile on without too much searching, and settled in for a long ride. McCoy had slowed his horse here, the shortened strides indicating that the animal was tired or that McCoy was holding it back, knowing that the cavalry had retreated.

The black smoke rose into the clear blue morning air like an accusing finger jabbing skyward. Ruff frowned and whipped the buckskin sheath from his Spencer repeater, and with his knees, he coaxed his horse into a run.

That was no campfire.

He was in an area of drift sand and dark hills, and when he emerged from the hills, he saw the burning wagon, the people behind it with guns blazing, the party of Indians working their way up the draw toward them, firing as they approached.

There were dead on the ground and in a moment another joined them as Ruff Justice, bringing his Spencer to his shoulder, triggered off from the back of his charging horse. It was a lucky shot on the run, as there hadn't been a lot of time to sight as the Apache leapt toward the barricaded whites. Ruff's .56 bullet, 500 grains of it, ripped into the Indian's chest, hurling him back like a mule kick.

Ruff stopped his horse and fired from its back. The animal had seen warring before, and it stood still, flinching only a little as the big, flat-shooting buffalo gun roared.

The Spencer took down another white-clad Apache and possibly a third, though the last one may have dived for the shelter of a gulley and escaped. Two Apaches with Winchester rifles fired at Justice, but their shots were very wild, almost panicky, and after a shot apiece, they fled.

And then all was still. The desert was soundless, except for the wind that whined and complained in the gulleys. The Apaches were nowhere to be seen. On horseback or afoot, they had been swallowed up by the desert sands or blown away by the wind.

Ruff started forward toward the burning wagon. He lifted his rifle high, and the gesture was answered by a summoning wave. He walked the buckskin toward the survivors.

He saw three Mexican men, two of them in fancy black suits with flat-crowned hats. The third was a half-Indian brute of a man in a torn red shirt.

The woman he saw last.

She emerged from the ditch where they had been sheltered, dusted her hands together, and walked forward to join the men. She was young and well put together. Firm, round breasts strained against the material of her white blouse. Her legs were long, and her silky black hair, free of its tortoiseshell comb, fell to her waist. Her eyes were black, frankly curious but strangely calm, considering what she had just been through. Her mouth was a little too wide, the underlip a trifle full. The corners turned up slightly in a brief smile.

Justice swung down from his horse, and cradling his rifle in his arms, he walked up to the men who were watching the wagon burn.

"Thank you," the older of the two men in suits said. His accent was heavy. He was silver-haired, dignified, aristocratic. "Thank you so very much. I do not know if we would have beaten them back again. I am Don Carlos Aguilar. My son, Ramón."

"Ruff Justice," the scout said, nodding to the younger man, who wore a thin mustache and a haughty, challenging expression on his dark face. Ruff waited expectantly, but no one introduced the woman.

There was no sense in being shy. He asked her directly, "Are you all right, señorita?"

"Yes. Thank you." She too had an accent but not as thick, and when she answered Ruff, she spoke slowly, drawing out the words provocatively. Her eyes expressed much, but Ruff wasn't sure he understood their meaning. "Thank you, Mister Justice, is it?"

"Ruff Justice, that's right."

"My name is Dolores. My father and brother do not introduce me to strangers. It is not our way, you see."

"I understand," Ruff said. Aguilar and his son were glowering, but whether it was at the loss of life and their goods, or at the heat of the day, or at Justice's lack of manners, Ruff just didn't know.

The big Indian had returned. His face was smudged, his forehead gashed and bleeding slightly. He reported in Spanish, "The horses are gone, Don Carlos, all but the señorita's black horse, which is standing in the arroyo to the south."

"Get it then," Ramón Aguilar said sharply.

"I mean to, Don Ramón," the big man said with just a shadow of irony, "but I did not wish to go without my rifle. There still may be Apaches out there, no?"

Ramón didn't answer; he merely looked bored.

Looking at the two aristocrats, Justice considered the familiar pattern: the dignified, solid father and the profligate, haughty son. There is something intrinsically crippling about spending another man's money, Ruff thought, especially if it happens to be your father's.

"I'll ride on down with you," Ruff offered. "Or I can make a circle and see if I can find your other horses. Maybe the Apaches didn't get off with all of them. They might have just scattered."

There was a long silence. These people didn't want Justice in their business.

The wagon collapsed with a crashing sound and a cloud of black smoke. They all glanced briefly in that direction.

Then the big man looked to Don Carlos, wanting to know if he should accept the American's offer of help. Don Carlos shrugged. *"Bien. Gracias,"* the big man said to Ruff. "I do not think the Apaches have gone far."

His name was Cacto—cactus—he told Ruff. He had never had another name. His mother was Opata Indian, his father a roving Mexican vaquero. Both had abandoned him, and the Don Carlos had taken him in.

"Where does he live?" Ruff asked from his horse. Cacto was walking beside him as they approached the huge black stallion that stood with its head bowed, saddle upside down, and one foreleg lifted as if it were injured.

"Don Carlos?" Cacto answered as if anyone but a madman would know. "On the Rancho Paseo Prieto."

"Where's that?"

"In the mountains, señor, in the mountains."

Ruff, who had spent some time down this way, just shook his head. He'd never heard of the rancho or its owner, nor imagined anyone but Apaches lived in the rugged, nearly impenetrable mountains.

"Stepped on a cactus, I think," the half-breed told Ruff as he reached the black horse. Justice looked carefully around the seemingly empty desert while Cacto worked at the animal's hoof, finally extracting a huge barrel-cactus spine.

"He all right?" Ruff asked.

"He is fine, yes, *gracias.*"

"There seems to be a buggy of some sort down in the gulley," Justice said, pointing ahead, squinting into the blinding sun.

"Yes, the other carriage—the one in which the señorita and her *dueña* traveled."

The carriage was on its side, one yellow wheel spinning lazily in the light breeze. The *dueña*, Dolores' chaperone and companion, lay pinned under the wagon, dead.

Cacto made a sharp, hissing sound and then sighed. "We can bury her there, if we can cave the bank in," he suggested.

"They won't want to take her home?" Ruff asked. It was a long, hot journey, but many people would have wanted to try. Cacto just shook his head.

They carried the woman a little way along the wash and laid her down at the base of a sandy bluff. Then they collapsed the bank on her, covering her. She could sleep that long sleep safe from the coyotes now.

They uprighted the buggy and hitched the black horse to it with a makeshift harness, as the Apaches had cut the original harness when they had taken the two horses pulling the buggy.

"Matched bays, very fine animals," Cacto said sadly.

The half-breed climbed into the box and started the black horse. He was still limping, and unused to a harness, it fought the idea all the way. The buggy lurched along, and Justice followed behind on his horse. Ruff wondered how these three people were going to make the mountains in a rickety buggy pulled by a crippled horse. The Apaches would likely come back and finish the job. But Justice had his own cats to skin. He couldn't be responsible for everyone he ran across. He'd given them some help, and now they were going to have to be on their own. Despite the dark-eyed, beautiful woman, he was going to have to turn his back on them and go after Dutch McCoy.

And that's the way it would have worked out, if the box filled with gold coins hadn't fallen from the buggy and spilled its rich load onto the desert sand.

3

Ruff pulled his horse up and sat staring at the gold, which lay scattered across the sand. He started to get down, and had his leg halfway over when Ramón Aguilar drew his pistol. "You hold it there, Señor Justice," he said, pointing the gun at Ruff. "And please drop your rifle before I kill you."

"Ramón," Don Carlos objected.

"Quiet, Father. You see how it is. Drop that rifle, Justice."

The cold, deadly tone of Ramón's voice made his demand seem like a good idea. Ruff dropped the Spencer and finished swinging down.

"Cacto!" Ramón shouted, and the half-breed with a shrug moved to Justice and lifted his pistol and bowie knife.

"This is stupid," Dolores said.

"Is it? He saw the gold, didn't he?" Ramón snapped.

"So what? He would not have known—"

"He saw the gold!"

"And now what are you going to do with him, eh?" Dolores demanded.

"I do not know. Kill him, maybe."

"No!" Don Carlos' voice was strong and authoritative. "I will not hear talk like that. This man saved your life, and mine, and Dolores'."

"Who asked him to ride in here? We had the Apaches beaten," Ramón said.

"The question remains: what can we do with him?" Dolores asked, looking Ruff up and down with what appeared to be amusement. "Take him home, perhaps?"

"Do not be absurd," Ramón spat.

"Then?" she challenged.

"Leave him here," he suggested.

"That's the same as killing him. The Apaches—"

"He has shown himself to be a fighter. You know the desert, eh, Justice?" Ramón asked.

Ruff didn't feel inclined to answer. The woman had been right—leaving him there afoot was the same as murdering him. Except the executioner didn't have to view his dirty work when it was done. But it still was murder, and by far a slower, more painful murder than a bullet through the head.

"We have to decide soon. If we do not leave now, we will never make the rancho by dark. Father?"

"Leave him," the old man said, turning away so that he wouldn't have to look Justice in the eye. "Cacto, pick up the gold."

"Yes, Don Carlos."

"You're going to let them do this?" Ruff asked Dolores.

"Me? How can I do anything about it?" she asked, smiling brightly. She was as cold as the others, it seemed. Ruff was mentally kicking himself for coming to their help. What had he stumbled onto? Whatever it was, it was worth killing for—at least Ramón figured it was. The man was actually grinning, damn him, with one corner of his lip curled back in amusement. The gun in his hand was steady.

"Cacto, get his horse."

"Sí, Don Ramón."

The buckskin was led away and backed into harness beside the black. Neither horse looked comfortable there, but they would do their job.

"Get in the buggy," Ramón said to Dolores, and with a last regretful look at Ruff, she did so. Cacto climbed into the driver's seat, and the worried-looking old don seated himself to wait for his son.

"Good luck, Ruff Justice," Ramón Aguilar said nastily. Then he backed away, climbed into the buggy, and as Cacto snapped the reins, the four of them rolled away, leaving Justice behind alone, unarmed, and afoot in the roughest country in the world.

Ruff spent a long minute cursing the desert. He had never had any luck on it. Sandfire had eluded him for months and now it appeared that Dutch McCoy had done the same thing. It looked as if that was the good luck—it didn't take a lot of imagination to realize what kind of shape Justice was in now. He was fifty miles into Sonora without a drop of water or a bit of food, unarmed except for the skinning knife in his boot sheath, surrounded by hard country and Apaches.

Maybe with luck a man could walk out alive, make the border—but only with luck. And only if the Apaches didn't find you. Ruff looked northward toward the border, then turned his head and stared at the tracks the buggy had cut into the white sand, tracks that pointed toward the far mountains, deeper into the desert of Sonora, deeper into Apache country.

He started walking. South.

They had his horse, and they had left him to die. Dolores was beautiful, but she wasn't beautiful enough to be forgiven this. She would pay—they all would.

The sun was rising higher now, growing hotter, blinding. Justice trudged on, following the wagon tracks, now and then seeing a distant dark speck that was the buggy, until it eventually disappeared into the horizon. At noon there was no shade for miles, and it was entirely too hot to walk on. The sun made men mad, and Justice had seen the sun bore into a man's brain and broil it so that the man had to be shot down like a mad dog.

A pale shadow crossed his face, and glancing to his right, Ruff saw an ironwood tree, so called because the wood is so hard it has to be harvested with a sledgehammer and not with an ax. The roots of an ironwood never rot and the wood burns hot and long. Just then, Ruff couldn't have been less interested in the tree as a source of fuel. It offered shade, fragile, lacy shade, and he sagged at the base and stared out bleakly at the desert.

The day moved past on heavy feet. Justice watched it through a swarm of spots that swam before his eyes. Half of them were colored, swirling, ephemeral. The other spots were gnats, risen from somewhere to form a living cloud around his head, filling his ears, nostrils, and eyes.

Justice batted at them with his hands, but it didn't do much good. He busied his mind, trying to figure out why Don Carlos had had so much gold with him, where he might have gotten it, where it was going . . . But his thoughts led him nowhere.

He was thirsty, so thirsty that his mouth's membranes seemed to have turned to cardboard, and his tongue to have swollen. And it was only the first day. How long would he last without water?

Long enough to exact retribution from Ramón Aguilar, who had thought nothing of leaving him out here to die of dehydration.

Ruff tried to push the heat from his mind. He thought of the northern mountains; of the winter he and the Crow woman, Four Dove, had been snowed in for three weeks; of her softly swaying breasts touching his chest as she straddled him and bent low to kiss his mouth, her dark hair forming a soft curtain . . .

Like some tasteless intruder, the heat forced the thoughts away. Justice glowered. He'd had enough. He got to his feet and started on, trudging through the sand, which soon became dotted with clumps of white sage and charamatraca, a slender cactus with roots like sacks of membrane filled with yellow fluid. Very good for backaches, the Indians said, and for compresses. But not nourishing at all.

He dipped down into a gravel-bottomed arroyo and followed it southward, knowing that there—if anywhere—he might find green plants and possibly water. There was nothing for miles but mesquite and nopal cactus, but that was saving for Justice. Mesquite beans, although bitter and flavorless, would provide nourishment; the pulp of the nopal would provide moisture.

He scavenged for the beans, shoving some in his mouth as he worked his way around the thorny bushes in the river bottom. He apologized to his buckskin horse for making it eat such poor fodder.

He had gathered a small pile of beans when he

finally sat down and began stripping the nopal pads of their thorny hide, chewing on strips of pulpy flesh cut from the inside. Once he got a thorn in his lip and uttered a profound curse.

He spent an hour in the wash, filling his body with moisture stolen from the nopal. But he couldn't remain there, living primitively off the land. He had to go on—there were people ahead he owed a debt to.

He started walking again, his legs knotted, his feet burning. The wagon tracks still cut twin, parallel grooves in the sand, still aimed directly toward the mountain where the Rancho Paseo Prieto lay hidden.

"Damn funny," Ruff breathed. "I never heard of that ranch or of the Aguilars."

Not that he had been everywhere in Sonora nor knew the land intimately as Sandfire and his people did, but men talked, and there were few secrets in this part of the country. Yet the Rancho Paseo Prieto—whatever, wherever it was—remained a secret. And it was filled with its own secrets, apparently. Secrets that gleamed like gold.

"Tough to figure," he muttered.

Ruff could see taking the gold out of the desert—to stash in a bank or purchase goods, although there was a hell of a lot of it for only that—but why bring it in when it was useless on the desert?

To conceal it? Why? Because it belonged to someone else?

Ruff shook his head. He didn't have enough information to guess at the answers. He didn't really care about the gold, never had. He cared only about the people who had left him to die. And it looked like there was a good chance of that now ... Ruff had spotted the mounted Apache half a mile back.

The Indian was keeping his distance, but he was definitely following Ruff, as Justice had determined when he deliberately veered from his southward course for a time.

The Apache was coming and he was armed. He had a war lance and in all likelihood a firearm. He wanted Ruff Justice. Wanted his hair ... Well, maybe not. Although it wasn't unknown by any means, Apaches weren't great ones for taking scalps. However, Ruff didn't find much consolation in knowing that his corpse might be left with all its silky locks.

Ruff glanced at the implacable Indian, still half a mile or so behind him, and then looked to the skies, urging sundown on, believing that after dark he would have a much better chance of eluding the Apache.

Ruff was out of the sand now, but the walking only grew more difficult, with rocks and cactus, sudden arroyos, and clumps of dry gray brush too thick to penetrate.

The Apache was still back there.

The sky seemed to dim slightly, and looking up, Ruff saw with surprise and relief that the sun was beginning to fall toward the horizon. He went on. He had his skinning knife in his hand, though what good the slender, razor-sharp knife would be against a rifle or handgun he couldn't have said. Yet he felt protected. He dipped down into a wash and found the dead willows.

They all stood at the same, tilted angle. Maybe a flash flood had uprooted them or a hard wind had tipped them over. But there they stood, shoulder to shoulder, all at a forty-five degree angle. Ruff looked back again, and then went to the willows, muttering to himself. He found the branch he wanted—slender, eight feet long—and he cut it free with his knife.

Then, still muttering, he looked up toward the rim of the arroyo, where the dark earth cut a strong, nearly straight line against the coloring sky.

Ruff started down the arroyo, moving at a quick trot now, surprised his body could respond to his wishes. He ran a quarter of a mile through brush and over rocks, and then clambered up to lie flat against the earth, only his eyes moving as he stared northward through the brush.

From his position, Ruff could see only the head of the Indian. His hair was nearly as long as Ruff's, hanging over his bare chest and shoulders. He wore white trousers made of manta, a light canvas favored by Indian traders for its inexpensiveness and by the Indians for its near indestructibility. Winking through the notch in the mountain, the sunlight gleamed brightly on the Apache's war lance.

The warrior knew something was happening, but he didn't know exactly what. The white man had gone into the arroyo but had not emerged on the far side. He could be hiding in the bottom—even sleeping, if he had been so inattentive not to have seen the following Apache. He could also have seen the Apache and decided to try to circle and attack. That seemed unlikely because the white man had no weapon, or at least no gun. Could he have hurt himself climbing down? the Indian wondered. That was possible. All the same, the Apache was in no hurry to go into the arroyo to see what had happened.

He, too, glanced at the sky and did not like what he saw. Soon it would be dark, and with no moon, the hunt would become impossible. He did not want to abandon his pursuit of the quarry. He was a young man and wished to prove himself.

He slipped from his pony's back and started forward, drawing from his wasitband the pistol his uncle had taken from a dead soldier the previous month. He left his lance in the ground. He would not need it, and it would be difficult to maneuver through the brush with it. The white man's pistol suited the warrior better.

He felt confident but also wary. The sky was going dark too rapidly. Flame red and orange-gold massed above the black mountains; the shadows beneath the bushes merged. Hearing a small sound, the warrior stopped and crouched, looking carefully to either side and then behind him. But nothing unusual was there— only the small creatures, the tiny ghosts that come alive with the darkness and amuse themselves by whispering words of fear in a warrior's ear.

He started on once again, still feeling uneasy, still hearing the night voices. They whispered their song to him, and he knew they spoke the truth this time. Someone would die before the dawn returned.

4

The Apache was nearly to the arroyo. He stood for a long while looking down into the deep shadows, watching for movement and listening for any whisper of sound, the breathing of an anxious man. But he heard nothing. Looking toward the mountains and then in the opposite direction toward the flats, he saw no one. He bit his upper lip and then went down into the wash, wanting to do this deed before dark, to ride back to the rancheria with the long-haired man as a trophy, with the hair of a dead white to boast over. Only then could he eat a man's meal, sleep in the warrior's wickiup, dance at the war festivals. The pistol was cool in his hand. The sky was surrendering to the darkness of the ages. The warrior slid into the brushy arroyo.

Justice saw him go down, and he was up in an instant, weaving through the brush in a crouch, his willow branch in his hand. His only interest now was the Indian's pony. If he could get on the horse and move out of there before the Apache emerged from the wash, he would be not only out of danger from the Indian, but also much closer to catching up with the Aguilar family and hopefully with Dutch McCoy, although by now McCoy's trail was beginning to get cold.

But it wasn't to be.

The warrior, summoned by some sound, reappeared, pistol in hand. Seeing Ruff Justice racing toward his horse, the Indian fired two-handed, and the pistol exploded in the silent desert, spewing flame as the slug covered the space between the Apache and Justice quicker than thought.

Hearing feet in the brush, Ruff had half-turned and started to hurl himself to one side. All of it was a split second too slow. The bullet whipped through the flesh beneath Ruff's left arm, tearing a deep, bloody groove between his ribs and taking a chunk of back muscle with it when it flew off into the darkness.

Justice hit the ground writhing in pain, biting his lip to fight back the cry of damnation. He felt woozy but had sense enough to keep rolling into the brush as the excited and overeager Apache placed two more shots toward the clump of sage where Ruff had first gone down.

The Indian's pony rose on hind legs and whickered angrily, frightened at this man's game and not wanting to be any part of it. The sky was dark but for a single orange ribbon above the hills and a light sprinkling of stars in the east. The horse backed nervously as the Indian neared Ruff's position, still wary but confident in his kill.

Ruff Justice lay in the brush, his hair in his eyes, blood leaking from his side onto the sand below, both hands wrapped tightly around his crude willow lance. The Indian came on, and Ruff blinked furiously, trying to rid his eyes of the burning, vision-blurring perspiration.

The Apache came nearer. Ruff watched the tall boots and the white pants as the Indian moved through the brush, his pistol thrust out in front of him defensively.

Slowly Justice drew one leg up under him, preparing himself. It was a painful and incredibly slow move, but finally he had done it. He wiggled his fingers on the shaft of willow, wondering how the weapon was going to defeat a Schofield pistol.

The warrior grew worried. The white man had disappeared, and yet he knew he had hit him. At least he thought he had hit him badly. He should be lying on the ground dead or dying, moaning piteously.

But he was not there. The paint pony stood looking at his master and shuddering with distaste. The sky had gone completely dark. The stars were bright and cold. He was not there.

Where, then? the Apache wondered. Where was the long-haired man?

He had to be in the brush, wounded and unarmed. The young warrior had been warned about pursuing injured men into the brush and into rocks, but he was not thinking clearly now—he only knew he wanted his kill, wanted to return home with news of his victory, to dance the war dance, to feast with the men . . . He stepped into the brush, and Ruff Justice rose from the dead.

The Indian's pistol exploded as he stepped back, the bullet whipping past Ruff's ear as flame spewed from the muzzle of the revolver. Justice's weapon was much slower than the bullet, but more effective. It was well-aimed, well-timed.

Ruff raised the willow pole high before driving it into the Apache's belly and ripping upward. The Indian uttered a strangled cry and tried to wriggle free.

But it was already too late for that; he was dying and he knew it. The pistol had been lost in the attack, and the Apache could do nothing in retaliation but strike out futilely with bloody hands before the life flowed from him and he collapsed to the earth at Ruff's feet.

Justice slumped to the ground to join him, feeling half-dead himself. The wound on his side was beginning to take a toll. He tried to rise, putting his hand on the Apache's chest, but he slipped down again. That wouldn't do, he thought. He had to get up, to get moving before the Indian's friends came looking for him. If they found Ruff there with the body, he wouldn't be dealt with mercifully, and the Apaches knew some tricks that made death seem desirable.

Ruff thought he could see the Indian's pony standing in the darkness a little way off. He needed that horse, wanted it badly. He also wanted the pistol the Apache had been carrying, but a search of the area failed to turn it up. The Apache must have hurled it a long way, Ruff decided.

The horse eyed Ruff Justice warily as he approached, speaking softly in a strange tongue, stretching out a hand for the hackamore knotted around the pony's jaw.

"Stand still now, you pretty thing . . . That's it. I won't hurt you. We'll go where the grass is long and sweet . . ."

Then Ruff had the hackamore, and although the pony shook its head vigorously a few times, he had himself a horse.

Mounting the animal was a different matter. Ruff lifted his left arm and nearly blacked out from pain. He leaned against the pony, blinking his eyes, staring at the swirling stars.

There had to be a better way to do it. But there wasn't—none that wouldn't hurt. In the end, he just grabbed a handful of mane and hoisted himself up, his mouth opening in a soundless cry.

"You're up. Now what are you going to do, damn you, Mister Justice?" he asked himself.

There was no good answer to that question. The border was much too far away, too far to even consider. He couldn't stay where he was, and if he went on, he only moved deeper into Apache country and nearer to Aguilar's rancho—wherever that was.

"Do something," Justice muttered. "Just *move*." He needed a place to hole up, a place where he might be able to heal a little. The Indian had a waterskin tied to his pony's neck, though he had no other provisions. If Justice could just find a cave, a high valley, a hidden canyon: anything that would offer concealment for a time . . . He started the horse forward into the night and the empty desert.

Ruff's head bobbed as he rode. At times he grew very confused, not knowing in what direction he was heading, why he was riding, or who in hell he was. Some absurd song about a three-legged woman kept ringing in his head.

Ruff fell from the pony's back, and as he lay there groaning, the horse looked down at him with bewildered eyes—its last owner had never done that. Justice lay there a long while, holding his side and watching the misty stars swing by, before he rolled over and got on hands and knees. Finally he got to his feet and stood looking at the animal, whose back seemed a hell of a long way up.

But Ruff got up there somehow. When he rode on again, there was a strange glow in the sky, and after ten minutes or so, he remembered what a moon was. That was as straight as his thinking got for a long while. There was the pony, the long, moon-glossed desert, the leaking of blood from the throbbing wound in his side, and a lot of other thoughts or illusions that had no meaning as they swirled and twisted and swam across his perception. Fiery feathers and long-necked bison with human faces; ghostly cavalry charges and long lines of female dancers cloaked in feathers and rain . . .

Ruff suddenly realized that he was no longer on the horse. He had fallen again, and this time he knew he wasn't going to get up. Where was he? he wondered. He could see canyon walls, dark and feature-less overhead; smell sage and distant cedar. The horse had gone and left him. Sheer desertion. Ruff began dragging himself toward a stack of rocks behind him. The protection probably didn't matter, as he must have been leaving a trail a child could follow, but he didn't want to be out in the open when they came.

And he had a feeling they would come soon.

They would come, and he would be lying there, crippled and unarmed, and that would be that. The moon was bright and the night was cold. He spent some time thinking about his past sins before he passed out, falling into a dreamless void.

When he awoke, there was frost on the ground. The little patch of grass beneath his face was silver with the stuff. The moon was gone and a pale glow in the east promised a sun soon.

Ruff tried to sit up, and his head felt like it was filled with molten metal. He lay back down, gingerly.

A century or two later he actually managed to sit up and look around. He was on a mountain trail, high up in a dark, probably nameless canyon overlooking the desert. Ruff figured the horse, or his own instincts, had brought him here searching for safety. He looked around carefully, seeing nothing and no one on the broad land.

The horse had managed to lose the waterskin, and it lay near the trail some thirty feet away. As badly as he needed that water to relieve the caked thirst in his throat, Ruff doubted he could make it that far.

But he started out. His body needed fluid. He crawled the distance, pausing to rest three times, panting and gasping as he dragged himself forward with only his good right arm. It seemed as if it took most of an hour to reach the waterskin and return to the boulders.

Once concealed again, he sat savoring the water, putting a few pearly drops on his tongue, rolling it around his mouth, and feeling his deprived body respond eagerly. Then he took a look at his wound.

It was puckered and a nasty red. Bruised skin surrounded the area where the bullet had grooved Ruff's ribs. He still had his skinning knife, and with that he cut both sleeves from his shirt and made a bandage. Trying to tie it was incredibly difficult, but Ruff finally made a reasonably satisfactory knot. Exhausted, he leaned back against the rocks and passed the day sipping water and dozing.

When he awoke, it was raining.

It seemed incredible. The morning had been cloudless, the sky clear, but thunderheads had slipped over the dark mountains and the cool rain fell.

That would make the tracking more difficult, Ruff thought, assuming there were any Apaches looking for him, warriors who had by now found their dead companion's body and started out after Justice. Thinking like that caused Ruff to lift himself up a little and try to see down the backtrail, but the clouds had filled the canyon and he could see nothing. He contented himself with filling the waterskin to the brim from a tiny rivulet running down the rock above him.

Somehow he fell asleep again, and when he awoke, he was soaked through. It had stopped raining, and the stars were out. The night seemed to be cold, almighty cold, but Justice was burning up.

He was on fire. His eyes opened, and he stared at the stars, feeling his teeth chatter as the rest of his body flamed with fever.

He drew his knees up and lay there, staring at the dark shapeless shadows, and then finally at the rising moon, as the night passed by, leaving him lost in pain and fever.

When she came, her hand was cool against his forehead, and her hair was soft against his cheek. Her breath was gentle, and she emitted worried little gasps interspersed with words in a language Ruff didn't understand.

She tried once to move him and gave that up. There was strength in her arms, but not that kind of strength. Who was she? he wondered. What did she want? Was she a death angel or the Crow woman come to take him back to the northlands?

After gathering twigs, she struck together flint and

stone. Justice wanted to tell her not to do it, not to build a fire, which would call his enemies, but his tongue wouldn't accept the message from his brain and he could only lie there watching the flames begin to curl and wink brightly in a golden dance. He could see her now, a young Indian, crouched over the fire, feeding it strips of bark from the brush around them.

Most of the border people knew some Spanish, and so Ruff tried to communicate with her.

"*Gracias.*" Justice uttered the word painfully.

Her head slowly turned toward him, and her hand touched his feverish forehead again.

"*Gracias,*" he repeated.

She didn't answer. Instead she walked away into the night, and for a time Ruff thought she was gone for good. But she returned, and with a sheet of canvas and two poles she built a rough shelter. Minutes later, it began to rain again. Ruff lay under the canvas covering, staring at the rain, the woman, and the curlicues of bright fire until they all merged into a fiery image of an angel of salvation.

5

When he awoke again, it was bright daylight and she was still there. Her presence made no sense, as one might expect these heavenly apparitions at night, in a delirium, but not in the daylight, not in the flesh. And she was definitely flesh and blood. In fact, she was a very pretty young woman with a nose too narrow for a border Indian, wide round eyes that glanced softly at Justice, a generous mouth, and a grace of movement uncommon and unexpected.

"You are awake again?" she asked in near-perfect English.

"I think so." He tried to move, and she put a hand on his shoulder, warning against such an action, as a wave of dizziness swept over Ruff, clouding everything for a brief moment.

There was a bandage and a poultice on his wounded side. He sat up slowly and watched her hazily as she brewed sycamore bark in a metal pot over the fire, making a tea that she poured for him soon afterward. The liquid was pale pink, very lightly flavored, and warming.

"Who are you?" Ruff Justice asked.

"The woman who lives here." She shrugged. "Better I should ask you who you are."

"You are Papago?" he asked.

"My mother was a Papago Indian." That seemed to be all she wanted to say on that.

"Your name?"

"What does it matter?" she replied.

"You saved my life—it matters."

"Toybo." She turned her eyes down as she told him her name, as if there were something immodest about it. "What is yours?" she asked after a short time.

"Ruff Justice." He handed her the clay teacup, and she refilled it.

"How do you feel now, Ruff Justice?"

"Weak. More comfortable, though. The fever's broken, I think."

"*Yerba del manzo*," she said. "It is very good medicine."

"What's on my arm now?"

"*Cardon* . . . You know what that is? Cactus. You must cut strips of it and tie it to the wound."

"You know a lot about medicine," he stated with interest.

Her dark eyes went to Ruff's and then shuttled away again. "Some. It is a thing I do for my people."

"Your people live here? In the canyon?" Ruff asked, surprised. He hadn't seen a more desolate, barren place in his life.

"Not far," she said ambiguously. "Rest now."

Ruff supposed that she wanted him to shut up, and so he did. Yawning, he leaned back against a rock, relishing the warmth of the new sun, the sun he had cursed and blasphemed for day upon day below on the desert.

He also watched the woman work. She was graceful, as he had noted earlier, and she concentrated on each small thing she did as if it were of the utmost importance.

Her lips moved, forming silent words, as she gathered fresh wood for the fire and stacked it inside the canvas tarpaulin. From time to time she caught Ruff's eyes on her and her lips formed words of disapproval.

It was hard not to watch her, however. She had an unusual length of limb, softly curving full breasts, and attractive hips concealed beneath a dark cotton skirt and blouse. In her hair, Ruff noticed, she wore a small ornament of turquoise. The figure of a hawk, he thought, or the Thunderbird.

"Why are you here?" she asked, still not looking at him. She had paused, half bent over, wood in her arms.

"I'm looking for a man who committed a murder. Where did you learn your English?"

"What man?" she said, ignoring his question.

"A man named McCoy."

"I do not know him."

"No. Toybo, tell me where you learned your English."

"At school," she replied. "A church school. You should not have come into the desert, should not have come into these mountains."

"It wasn't by choice," Justice assured her. "I killed an Apache and he wounded me. I took off. In the wrong direction, I guess. It was mostly the horse's doing. You haven't seen the horse, have you?"

"No." Her eyes had brightened. Putting the wood down, she scooted toward him on her knees. "You killed an Apache?"

"Yes."

"Just one?"

"Just the one, Toybo."

She reached out and clutched Ruff's forearm tightly for a moment. "You will kill more?" she said with some savagery.

"Only if I have to."

"They are all bad," she said, her hand falling away.

"Not all. They aren't all like Sandfire."

"Sandfire—filthy dog!" She turned her head and spat.

Ruff's eyes narrowed. "Do you know Sandfire?"

"Everyone in these hills knows Sandfire. All Papago Indians know Sandfire. How do you know him, Ruff Justice?"

"I was with the army, tracking him for many months. We didn't have much luck."

"If you find him?"

"Him," Ruff muttered thoughtfully. "I would kill him. Although just now I couldn't squash a bug."

"He has killed many people, many Papagos," Toybo said distantly.

"He doesn't roam this far east, does he?" Ruff asked, slightly worried.

"Yes. All the time. We watch for him. All of the Apaches are bad, very bad, but he is the worst. Last winter he burned our village because we would not give him our corn. Then when the fire got in his eyes, it stirred him to kill many of my people. We ran into the hills."

It was an old story and an unhappy one. The Papagos, Pimas, and other small tribes had been preyed on by the Apaches for centuries. There was so much animosity between these peoples now that there could never be a peaceful resolution, assuming anyone wanted one, which they didn't. They wanted only the blood of their enemies on their hands.

Toybo brought Ruff his waterskin, some mesquite flour cakes sticky with molasses, and a slender strip of venison. Ruff's stomach rumbled at the sight of the food, and he ate slowly but eagerly, alternating with sips of water.

Incredibly, when he finished, he was sleepy again. His body just didn't have many reserves left. He had come as close to the edge as possible without falling over. He really believed he wouldn't have made it if Toybo hadn't come out of the darkness to find him, to heal him.

"Isn't someone looking for you?" Ruff asked over a yawn. "Your family?"

"No family," she said sharply.

"No husband?"

"Go to sleep," she commanded, and he did, watching her for a minute, the stretch and sway of her body as she worked, the soft curves and purposeful lines of her. As Justice closed his eyes, her soft humming was in his ears. It was very nice, very peaceful.

It was dark when he awoke and found a hand on his mouth. Ruff started to strike out, but from the depths of his heavy sleep he recognized it as Toybo's hand. The night was black, crickets sang, and the stars were fat and richly glowing.

"What is it?" he whispered.

"Apache. Below us on the trail. Can you walk?" Her breath was hot and urgent on his ear, her eyes bright in the starlight. Her breasts nudged his chest as she bent low to speak to him.

"If I have to," he answered. He honestly didn't

know if he could but there wasn't much of a choice. It was either walk or die. He got up.

Toybo was under his right arm. His left, bound to his side by the Papago woman's bandage, was useless. "Cut the bandage," Ruff said.

"Your wound will open up."

"This is no good," he explained tersely. "I'll need my left arm."

She didn't argue. His bandage fell away, and pain rushed through his side and back as the poultice was removed. They started on, Toybo supporting him. They had to leave the tarpaulin behind, which was bad because it was easy for the Apaches to spot, but there hadn't been time to fold it, and Toybo wasn't going to carry Ruff and the canvas too.

They moved uphill as swiftly as possible. Ruff staggered and weaved. He kicked over a rock, and Toybo sucked in her breath, perhaps in disgust at this noisy wounded white man. Perhaps in sheer fear.

They went nearly straight up the canyon side, following a game trail through the chest-high brush. The moon was rising and Toybo glanced fearfully at it, for it would illuminate the wall of the canyon, and anything there would be visible to the searching eyes of the Apaches.

When they had gone as far as they could go, they lay on a small ledge, peering through the brush down toward the camp.

It wasn't good. Justice could see the Apaches now, moving afoot in single file up the trail from the desert. They were searching, definitely searching. No accident had brought them to the dark canyon. The moon peered over the craggy hills, and the tarpaulin Toybo had stretched for Ruff's roof was clearly visible, standing out from above like a white rectangle painted against the black background. They could only hope that, from below, it wouldn't catch anyone's eye.

The Apaches moved very slowly, scanning the ground for signs of their prey. Ruff would have bet that no one could track him after the rain, but the Apaches seemed to be doing just that—unless they were following Toybo. He glanced at her, and she just shook her head silently. But it didn't matter how they had gotten there or who they were after. They were there, and they would kill both of them if given the chance.

Ruff lay watching in taut silence. His hand had closed around a stone in some futile, primitive gesture of defiance.

The Apaches moved upward. Now they were within twenty yards of the camp. The moon, brighter each minute, beamed down on the tarpaulin. If they found the camp, Justice had no doubt they would find the tracks leading up to them, and he had no doubt as to the outcome of that. His stone just wasn't going to do the job against four armed Apaches.

He felt Toybo's hand rest on his arm, felt her grip tighten as the Apaches hesitated and then started on, following the trail up the canyon, past the camp. Ruff let out a long slow breath.

They didn't move for another half an hour as the Apaches rounded a bend in the moonlit trail and vanished.

"Come," she whispered in sharp command, and Ruff rose to a crouch. Toybo had already begun moving up the trail, not waiting to assist him now. There was no time, and the trail was too narrow for double climbing. Justice would have to keep up or else.

He tried his damnedest, but he was weak and his side hurt like hell. Toybo must have the eyes of a cat, he thought, for the moonlight was bright, but it didn't penetrate the thick brushy carpet they crept through as they climbed toward the far side of a pyramidal rock.

Ruff held his side and staggered on, only now and then allowing himself to look back down the trail, fearing what he might see.

He pushed himself forward, and somewhere the pain was left behind and replaced by a dreamy otherworldness through which he wandered, his heart swollen in his chest, his lungs filled with a light gas that buoyed him but made breathing difficult. He watched his feet for a time, watched them slide out in front of him and draw him along. He watched them until he fell on his face and lay there groaning.

"Get up, Ruff Justice," Toybo commanded. She crouched over him, her wide eyes tense and alert in the moonlight. She tugged on his arm and somehow managed to pull him to his feet, and they continued up the endless slope.

And then they were at the canyon crest. Standing there, chests heaving for breath, the chilly wind washing over them, Toybo and Ruff looked into the vast dark declivity at their feet.

"They do not come," Toybo said.

"No. Not now."

Not now, Ruff thought, but what about in the morning when they realize they had lost the trail and double back to look for it?

Toybo shook her head and they went on, moving

very slowly, almost disconsolately. Without Toybo, Ruff wouldn't have made a quarter of the distance. She knew the mountains, the trails, and the pitfalls. She was there to give him support when his wounds caused the dizziness to come rushing back. Going downslope, Ruff seemed worse than he had before, but now he was more tired and the loss of blood was more taxing.

He stumbled again and fell. It was a very bad place to go down, for below lay a sheer cliff face, perhaps three hundred feet high, with talus at its base. They were working their way across the trail above the slope, a narrow path no broader than a spread hand, when Ruff's foot slipped. Perhaps he had grown dizzy and missed his footing or maybe he had simply been inattentive, but he went down—and over.

He was suddenly clinging to the edge of the trail with both hands, his side screaming out with pain as he extended his left arm to hold on. Toybo clawed at his wrists, trying to brace herself, to pull Justice to safety, but she couldn't find a grip.

Ruff's boot toes scraped futilely at the face of the bluff, trying to find a small toehold, a crevice, an outcropping, anything to help himself up and over.

But there was nothing. His left arm wasn't much help to him any longer. He was falling. He could feel Toybo's fingers rake his wrists as he slid from her grasp.

Then his toe found something. It was little enough, only a small concavity, barely enough to wedge the toe of his boot in, but it allowed him to take the weight off his right hand, get another grip, and with Toybo's help, pull himself to the safety of the narrow trail.

"No more," he panted.

"You are a warrior?"

"So they tell me."

"Then you will not quit. Come now, we have a little way to go."

Then she turned and walked away, and there was nothing for Ruff to do but get up and follow her. He sure as hell wasn't going to make it on his own. With lungs, heart, and side aching, leg-weary and nearly stuporous, he went on.

It wasn't long before dawn when Toybo found the place she had been pointing them toward. Hidden in the folds of the hills was a high grassy valley where cedar and spruce grew. There was water flowing somewhere—Ruff heard it but could not see the source.

"This is an old place," Toybo said without explanation. Ruff didn't care if it was old or new. It was the end of the trail.

His enough to look down over the country they had just traversed, it was secluded and pristine. Toybo led Ruff through trees streaked with moisture and ghostly in the gray of predawn. When they had passed through the trees, they emerged into another, even smaller valley. Above this valley, past a stand of dead gray oaks, was the cave.

There was a little climb to it, but for Ruff it seemed like another mountain. Yet once having reached it, he found it worthwhile. The cave was dry, deep, and secure, overlooking all of the hillside below them, the hillside that was now bathed in the orange glow of dawn. Birds filled the skies above the dark pines.

"Sit," Toybo commanded with just a little derision. She apparently wasn't impressed much with Ruff's warrior's prowess. She slipped out of the cave, leaving Justice to sag to the stone floor and sit sipping water from the skin, watching sunrise alter and pale the world.

After a brief time, Toybo returned with her arms full of pine boughs with which she made a springy, aromatic bed. "Rest," she said when she was through.

"And what about you, Toybo, where is your bed?"

"My bed?" She frowned. "I will sleep with you, of course, Ruff Justice." And she began to remove her moccasins.

6

The sun was warm on their bodies. Ruff Justice lay looking at the even white part at the top of Toybo's head. She was cuddled beside him, sound asleep.

She hadn't been as close to him when Justice fell asleep. He had lain down and had been joined a minute later by Toybo, who immediately turned away from him and fell asleep—or feigned sleep. But during the morning human instinct had brought Toybo next to him, to place her small clenched fist on his chest and her cheek on her fist, to breathe softly as Ruff Justice watched the sun, already beginning to decline.

She seemed to feel his eyes on her and she lifted her head heavily, her unfocused eyes looking up into Ruff's face. Then she stiffened and sat upright, pushing away so hard that it hurt Ruff's side and he winced.

"What are you doing?" Toybo asked.

"Watching you sleep."

She didn't like the answer. Toybo rose and hurriedly pulled on her moccasins. "Someone should have been hunting. What will we eat? Someone should have been watching for the Apaches. Someone should see to your wound," she recited.

"You needed rest too, if you're the someone you're going on about," Ruff said, sitting up.

"I do not need rest. Not so much."

He couldn't argue with that. If she didn't need rest, then she wasn't human. After all, it had been a long, hard climb.

"First the wound," Toybo said. She went to Ruff, who sat on the bed, watching. "It is too early for deer to feed."

"Is that what you're going to get for us to eat—venison?"

"Yes," she said with assuredness. "I will make a bow and arrows. I know where the deer come for water."

She yanked at the bandage and Ruff felt scab tear away. He clenched his teeth and looked to the skies beyond the cave.

"Well? How's it look?"

"You heal well. It looks good. When I have killed a deer, I will make you medicine out of burnt antler. That will heal you quickly."

"What are you, a medicine woman or something?" Ruff asked.

"Sometimes. Some Papagos think I am a medicine woman."

"What do the others think?"

"The others?" Toybo looked at him and smiled crookedly. There was a distant light in her eyes. "The others believe I am a witch woman."

Ruff started to answer her smile with his own, but he realized suddenly that she wasn't joking. A strange little quiver moved up along his spine. He had a sharp remembrance of her appearing from nowhere out of the night to build a fire and tend his wounds . . . but that was all fantastic and Justice shrugged the thought away.

"I cannot bind the wounds. Leave them open to the air now. They will heal," Toybo said. She rose, wiping her hands on her black cotton skirt. She looked outside, at the long valley, the stand of spruce, the white desert beyond. "It is time for me to make ready for the hunt. You may gather wood, then watch for the Apaches. Look carefully."

"All right," Ruff said, a smile curling his lips. She was getting a little bossy now. Still he couldn't argue with success. She did save him from death and had led him out of the canyon in the darkness. And if they ate tonight, it would be only because Toybo hunted for them. If it were up to Justice, he would have simply rolled over and gone back to sleep for another twenty-four hours; he felt that battered.

Instead he got slowly to his feet and walked to the mouth of the cave to watch as Toybo worked her way down the slope and disappeared into the trees. Then with a shrug, Justice went out to gather what dead-wood he could find on the ground.

When he had a fair-sized pile up in the cave, he went out again and looked to the high ground just beyond the cave. A wind-twisted cedar jutted out precariously from the surrounding gray boulders. It was the highest accessible point for miles, and Ruff started climbing.

He didn't really have to exert himself, yet by the time he had reached the little promontory, he was physically defeated. He breathed deeply, raggedly as the cold wind washed over him. He could see for miles into the dark canyon, out toward the white playa, and to the dark southern hills where the Aguilar family supposedly had their rancho.

Recalling the Aguilars set his blood to boiling. He strained his eyes in the direction of the rancho, as if by looking hard enough he could be transported there to exact his vengeance.

"Cold-blooded bastards," he muttered. Thinking of the gold he had seen spilled on the sand, Ruff wondered once again why such a party traveled with so much money. Maybe by now the Apaches had the gold. That would have been fitting. Maybe they had run into Dutch McCoy, and he had appropriated it. No, if McCoy had any sense, he would have swung back across the border into the United States long ago, and was very likely sitting in Tucson smoking a big cigar and drinking a tall beer.

He saw no Apaches.

He searched the distances carefully. The clouds were gathering on the western horizon. It was rare to see two storms so close together on the Sonoran desert, but it looked very much like it would rain soon.

Down on the flats, too distant to make out anyone or anything clearly, Ruff saw no signs of movement— no dust clouds stirred by passing feet or animals. There was nothing on the trail leading back to the dark canyon. The Apaches either had gone on searching for the trail or perhaps had never been looking for Justice at all. But from their movements, Ruff doubted that.

The sky was deep purple, the canyons deeply shadowed. A single star appeared bright and solemn above the horizon as Ruff returned to the cave, summoned by the smell of woodsmoke, and he thought, hopefully, of roast meat.

Toybo was there, and on a spit was a haunch of venison, dripping juices onto the fire below it. In the corner stood a bow and three makeshift arrows, headless, sharpened crudely, and featherless—but apparently deadly enough, accurate enough.

"You had luck."

She turned sharply. "It was not luck."

"All right."

Toybo looked at him, her eyes softening. Then she shrugged. Ruff crouched down to watch her. He wondered what she was doing out here alone, where her people were, where she had learned English, why some of the Papagos believed she was a "witch woman." There were no answers in her dark eyes, in the twisting flames, in the swaying and dipping of her body as she tended her venison.

She cut a slab of meat for him from the outside of the haunch, and Ruff ate with an incredible appetite. They had the roasted venison, water, and a few flour cakes that were left from Toybo's provision bag.

Stuffed and satisfied, Ruff leaned back against the wall of the cave, and with his hands folded on his lap, watched the flickering flames paint patterns on the wall and across the Indian woman's face.

"What happened, Toybo?" Justice asked finally.

"What do you mean?" She did not look at him.

"Why are you out here in these hills alone? Where are the rest of your people, and why aren't you with them?"

"Because I am a witch woman," she answered.

"Sure."

"It is true," she said sadly, as if admitting a shameful failing.

"Did they tell you that—or did you tell them?" Ruff Justice wanted to know.

"What do you mean?"

"I mean just what I said. Why do you think you're a witch woman? Is it because of things they've told you, or is it because of some idea you've got in your head on your own, something you went around trying to convince everyone of?"

"Why would I *want* to be a witch woman!" she cried.

"I don't know." There was a long silence. The meat continued to hiss and trickle juice, even though the fire had gone to golden coals. The cave was very warm.

"It is just the truth," Toybo said.

"It's the truth that you're a witch?"

"Yes."

"Listen, tell me the whole story. I don't understand much of this. Were you born a witch woman, birthed under a shooting star? Did the owl call three times? What happened?"

"When I was three I was taken by the white soldiers," Toybo began. "This is how that happened. One night, while we slept in the valley, the old valley where the Papago had always lived, the Apaches came. They attacked in the night and drove us from our wickiups, shooting arrows into sleeping people.

"My uncle was a wise man called Snow Thought. He took me by the arm and we hid in a dry creek behind the camp. My mother was dead, though I did not know it then. The Apaches had killed her. All night fires burned. All night I could hear Apaches talking in their strange tongue. My uncle pressed me to the ground, and when the Apaches came too near, he would hold his hand over my mouth, afraid that I would cry out in fear.

"With the morning they were gone. Everyone was dead. Snow Thought mourned and cut off three fingers with grief. Then he gathered up our blankets and a provision sack, and we walked out of the valley. He told me we would hide in the day and walk by night to the high valley where all the people would run, those who had survived. We did not walk far, however. The Apaches found us, and Snow Thought was killed fighting. I hid in the bushes and shivered, but the Apaches did not find me. They were so close I could have reached out and touched one's foot. His name was Sandfire."

"How'd you know that?" Ruff Justice asked.

"They spoke Spanish," she answered.

"Spanish? Wait a minute—you spoke Spanish at that age?"

"We all speak Spanish in Sonora. It is the tongue of the traders. All the Indians know it."

"All right." But why? he wondered. Why were the Apache raiders speaking Spanish? Unless the people they were speaking to weren't Apaches. "You saw the Apaches. You saw Sandfire. What else did you see?"

"Nothing. I buried my head in my arms. I did not look, I did not breathe."

"Then they went away and you were alone in the world," Ruff finished.

"We are all alone in the world. But yes, I was a child alone. I walked toward the high valley. I had a chance of making it without becoming captured—if the Apaches capture children from other tribes they sell them to the Mexicans for slaves."

"So I've heard."

"The Mexicans are fools. They think the Apaches are friends. The Apaches are simply cunning. They sell them children and then steal them back. The same as they do with horses and mules and cattle. There is warfare everywhere between the Apache and the Mexican, yet they try to use each other like this. On one side of the mountain Sandfire might kill and pillage and raid, and on the other sell back women and livestock he has stolen. The man in Chihuahua buys what has been stolen in Sonora, the man in Sonora what has been taken on the return trip from Chihuahua. These few evil men think they are cheating the Apache, but the Apache grows wealthy."

"Fortunately for you, the Apaches didn't find you."

"No. Or I would be serving tables in Chihuahua or being slut to some rich old man."

"Slut—the soldiers teach you that word?" Ruff asked with a smile.

"And many others." Toybo wasn't smiling. "They found me—American soldiers looking for Sandfire—and I went to them knowing that whatever they were, they were better than the Apaches. They took me to the reservation school and there I learned English."

"But you left."

"I ran away. But I knew English, I knew many things. On the reservation I had worked with the doctor. I knew white medicine and I knew Indian medicine. I wanted to heal . . ." She paused. "When you have seen much death and much pain, you wish to heal, Ruff Justice."

"Good people do, yes."

"I do not know about that. I just wished to heal. When I got back to my people, they were shocked. They had buried me in their minds, mourned for me."

"You had family left?"

"Old grandmother and my brother, Thei. My grandmother is dead now, but before she died, she taught me more medicine."

"All right. I understand all of this. You've had an interesting life. Maybe frightening, maybe very difficult. But what makes you a witch, Toybo?" he asked her.

A log fell, sending a spray of sparks into the air.

Toybo glanced in that direction. "The medicine, Ruff Justice," she answered, "the medicine made me a witch woman."

"I don't understand."

"I could heal everything. A broken bone, a bad stomach, a fever. Yet I was young. The people did not trust me. They said the whites had given me bad magic."

"You had white medicine with you?"

"Some. I took it when I left the reservation school. I used it sometimes. I grew proud. My brother gave me to a warrior."

"To marry?"

"We were going to be married, Iron Heart and I. After my medicine went bad, he turned his back on me."

"What do you mean your medicine went bad?" Ruff asked, but she wouldn't answer. There was only the faint whispering of the wind and the crackling of the low flames. "Toybo?" Ruff prodded. "What happened?"

"Nothing. Nothing happened," she said, and her eyes flooded with sudden tears, "except that I killed them all. Thirty people. Women and small ones and old warriors. I killed them all with my bad medicine!"

7

Ruff Justice stared across the fire at the girl. The woman who had had such a tumultuous early life, who had lived frightened and alone, who had seen the catastrophes man inflicts upon man, who had seen war and disease and imprisonment.

He shook his head. "You didn't kill anyone, Toybo. You know that."

"But I did!" she cried. "You were not there—you did not see it. You would not know."

"I know you."

"You do not know me at all!"

"Toybo." He put his hand on her shoulder, but she shrugged it away. "I know you're no killer."

"My magic was bad."

"Something went wrong. Something you couldn't help."

"I *caused* it. I caused death. I am a witch woman with evil ways, with the eye of death and . . ." Suddenly she was in tears again, and Justice scooted toward her. This time she let him hold her as she sobbed against his shoulder, and the fire burned low.

"What was it, Toybo?"

"The pox. Half of our people were sick with it. We have no medicine for the pox"—she sniffed and wiped angrily at her nose—"but the whites do. I know this because I saw the people on the reservation treated for the pox. Only three died. Out of many hundreds. I heard my own people crying for help. Children in the night. And so I decided to go for medicine."

"To the whites?"

"Yes. To a trader I knew who had medicine for sale," Toybo replied. She sat up and moved away from Ruff, sniffling a little. "My brother Thei and Iron Heart gave me many horses to sell, all of our tribe's wealth, and I took them to the trader. I waited two days for the medicine, and then we rode home swiftly.

"I gave the medicine to thirty people. To . . . thirty people. And of these thirty . . . every one died, Ruff Justice. That was how my medicine worked, how the woman who knew the pox killed her people."

Ruff was silent for a long while, watching the grief surface in Toybo, shake her body, and break loose the tears that trickled down her cheeks. She put a hand to her forehead, covering her eyes, and in a muffled voice said, "I wanted only to save them, to heal them." She sniffed loudly and sat up, sighing. "And so I was driven from the tribe."

"Your brother, your future husband . . ."

"Thei and Iron Heart turned their backs on me. I had squandered the tribe's wealth and killed many with my dark medicine. I was a witch woman."

"Something went wrong, that's all."

"There are reasons why things go wrong. Sometimes the small spirits do things. Sometimes the dark side of the universe turns toward you. Bad spirits caused the deaths, Ruff Justice. If they did not, then it was I who did it deliberately. I was a witch woman or a murderer. My brother told them that I was a witch so they would not kill me. A witch cannot help being evil. Besides, she has many dark spirit friends to strike back at those who would harm her, and so I was left alone."

There wasn't much to say. A woman from a primitive culture had learned just a little too much of modern medicine. Just enough to cause harm. People had died. She was a witch.

"The medicine may not have been good, Toybo."

"It was good. Señor Aguilar assured me of that. It was in sealed—"

"*Who?*" Ruff demanded. He shot upright and gripped Toybo's shoulders so tightly that he could see the pain in her eyes. He released his grip. "Who sold you that medicine?"

"Señor Aguilar. Aguilar is a friend of the Papago, who sells us what we need. Why . . . ?"

Ruff didn't answer. He simply shook his head, seeing those golden coins strewn across the sand, and imprinted on every one was the face of a dying Papago Indian.

"You know Señor Aguillar?" Toybo asked.

"I've met him."

"He has a beautiful daughter."

"Lovely." Ruff's mind turned one way and then the other, groping, trying to put things together. He had his suspicions about Aguilar, an idea as to why no one had ever seen his ranch, why it was a well-kept secret, why they had determined to leave Ruff Justice to die on the Sonoran desert.

"What is the matter? What are you thinking?" Toybo asked.

"I'm thinking that I'd like to know more about Aguilar."

"But why?"

"I think he's up to his hips in dirty business."

"What dirty business?" Toybo laughed. "He is an honorable man. You do not know him well."

"He trades with the Indians," he stated flatly.

"Yes."

"With all of them. Papago, Suma, Opata, Pima . . ."

"Yes, but—"

"And Apache?"

"I do not know, Ruff Justice. Perhaps." She absorbed that thought slowly, but didn't seem to give it much significance, except for the anger that rose every time she heard the word "Apache."

But Justice felt it had significance. What significance he didn't exactly know, but he thought that the Papago troubles, Aguilar, and the Apaches were all revolving around a common hub.

"I'd like to see that rancho of his," Justice said.

"But why? What buiness do you have with Aguilar?"

"Do you know where it is?" Justice asked, ignoring her question.

"Of course, but I do not understand this, Justice."

Briefly, he told her of his meeting with Aguilar and his children, of the Apache fight.

Toybo shook her head in confusion. "But if the Apaches were attacking him, then he is not their friend at all."

"Maybe not. I never considered him their friend, but only a business associate, and in these associations people get angry, they get greedy. Maybe Aguilar had cut someone out of some gold, out of horses, slaves—he must deal in slaves, too, right?"

"I have never heard that he did, but it is important business in Sonora."

"Yes. And if it's going on, I'd wager Aguilar is involved."

"But you assume so much, Ruff Justice."

"Maybe you're right. I know several things, however. The man is crooked and he's rich. He doesn't mind killing. He deals with the Indians. Mostly the Indian trade is in horses and livestock, sometimes in slaves, young children from either side of the border, or pretty women. The Apaches are the ones who specialize in the slave trade between here and the United States, between Chihuahua and Sonora. I assume a lot, maybe, but I think the man is dirty, very dirty. Even if he isn't into everything I'm guessing he's into, he's guilty of trying to kill me. Him and that flashy son of his and that black-eyed daughter."

"You would kill them?"

"Maybe." The fire was burning low. Ruff stared at it bleakly.

"Even the woman?" Toybo was nearer to him now and her hand rested on his shoulder. He glanced at her.

"I don't know, Toybo."

"You like women, do you not, Ruff Justice? Women who can lie down with you and share your blanket."

"I like them, Toybo."

Her eyes glittered in the pale firelight, her breathing lifted her breasts, pressing them against the cotton blouse she wore. "And me. . . ?" Toybo asked. "Do you like me?" She was hesitant but eager, her nostrils flared, her lips slightly parted.

She leaned intently toward Ruff Justice, and he took her hair at the back of her neck, gripped it, and bent her head back. His mouth found hers and searched it, tasting the damp sweetness of her. She clutched his thighs and a searching hand found his groin and began a gentle stroking.

"I think you are well enough," she said breathily. "Well enough . . ." And she crossed her arms and whipped her blouse off over her head. Her full, dark-nippled breasts bobbed free, lending themselves to Ruff's cupping hands, to his small, flitting kisses. He could feel her heart hammer, feel her hands on his shoulders, her breath against his cheek.

Slowly and carefully she removed his shirt. Then she slipped from her skirt by firelight and stood naked and lithe, long in the thighs, long in the waist, full-breasted, her hips gently swelling, the dark triangle between her thighs compelling. She stood over Ruff for a long minute as he ran his hands up the backs of her thighs, clenching her smooth, strong buttocks, and kissed her soft, rounded abdomen.

She knelt suddenly, and as Ruff lay back on the bed of pine boughs and Toybo's discarded garments, she unfastened his trousers and tugged them down with little grunts of concentration, effort, and anticipation. When she had them off, she cast them aside. Ruff, on his back, lay looking up at Toybo as she stepped forward and towered above him, straddling him. Ruff smiled and touched her legs, sending a quiver through her.

She dropped to her knees and shook her hair loose across Ruff's chest and shoulders. He stroked her hair, pulled her face to his, kissing her as Toybo's searching hand reached between Ruff's legs and found him. She positioned herself and slowly sank onto him, a little gasp of pleasure escaping her lips.

She settled onto him, arching her back and neck, looking into the infinite distances as pleasure consumed her. Slowly she began to sway, to work against Ruff, to reach between her legs and touch him where he entered her.

Then she leaned forward and kissed his chest, her breasts grazing his abdomen, filling her nipples with sensation. A warm, tingling need crept down across her stomach to her thighs and caused the liquid warmth there to increase, to swell and flow as she lifted herself and settled again, working her inner muscles as her lips searched Ruff's chest, neck, the line of his jaw, his eyelids, and forehead.

She moved against him, nudging him toward a climax with each urgent thrust of her pelvis. He still could feel the pain in his side and back, but the sensation building in his loins washed out the worst of it.

"You are a medicine woman, a good medicine woman," Ruff said, reaching between her thighs to feel her moisture. Her soft flesh caressed him, and he worked his fingers against her as she pitched and swayed, her teeth clenched tightly, her starry eyes bright and damp. The fire glossed her coppery flesh, outlining and shadowing her, making her breasts, abdomen, thighs, and shoulders works of art cast in bronze—moving, living bronze that no artist could compete with. "You are a medicine woman."

"Not witch woman?"

"Not a witch woman, no." Ruff stroked her arms and bent forward to kiss her breasts, to take a taut nipple between his teeth. Then he lay back, letting her work, watching her, feeling the need grow and threatening to burst within her.

"My magic is good?" she asked from a great distance. Her words and her body, mind and matter, seemed disconnected from each other. She spoke softly as her body continued its urgent, methodical pushing, its demanding caress.

"Good magic," Ruff replied. "It heals me, brings me to life, makes me rise and flow. Can't you feel the flow, the completion, the healing?"

"Yes," she whispered, and then her own completion, her own healing, shook her violently and she cried out before collapsing against Ruff, before clinging to him in the night with hot tears, causeless but necessary, spilling across his chest. Ruff held her and they slept.

When morning came, the Indians were there.

Justice tried to move but discovered that Toybo was still sprawled across him, her thigh over his, her arm across his chest.

There were five of them, all armed with ancient muskets and trade knives, all wearing cotton shirts and manta trousers. They wore their hair chopped off square in front and back; their leader wore a turquoise and silver necklace. He stepped into the cave, anger twisting his features. He swung his moccasined foot out and kicked Ruff Justice squarely in the ribs on his right side.

The wind went out of Ruff and he doubled up in agony as pain shot through him. Toybo, suddenly awake and alert, leapt to her feet, naked and proud, and hurled herself at the Indian.

He slapped her aside, and she skidded across the floor of the cave to lie still, curled up. Justice rose to his feet only to have the muzzle of a rifle shoved into his belly. The hammer was drawn back and the Indian looked as if he meant business.

"No, Iron Heart," Toybo cried, stretching a hand toward him.

"White bastard," the Indian said in Spanish.

"Leave him alone! Thei, I beg you!" Toybo shouted to another Papago. Ruff knew the names. He looked at Toybo's brother and the man she was to have married before her medicine went bad. They weren't his first two choices of men he would have wanted to meet just then. Ruff remained motionless, his hands half-raised, the chill of morning in his bones and the colder sensation of near death knotting his belly as Iron Heart jabbed the muzzle of the ancient rifle musket more savagely into Justice's stomach.

"You will die," the Papago said to lighten the atmosphere a little. Ruff believed him. He had seen men who were just talking when they said that; he had seen the deadly serious ones. Iron Heart was one of the latter.

Toybo was on her hands and knees, crawling toward her brother.

"Please, Thei, stop this!"

Thei was impassive. "Cover yourself, girl. Why do you shame me in front of my warriors?"

"Who is this?" Iron Heart asked. His eyes raked Justice, taking in the long, lean muscles, the battle wounds, the new, unhealed injury. He looked at the long dark hair, the drooping mustache, the loins of his white intruder. Then he jabbed the musket into Justice's belly still harder yet.

"Why are you doing this?" Toybo demanded. "You chase me from my people. You, Iron Heart, tell me I am not fit for your wife, and now you come in a jealous rage like a twelve-year-old because I slept with this man."

"This *white* man," Iron Heart spat.

"Yes, this white man. So what? At least he is a warrior." Ruff wished she hadn't said that as Iron Heart once again jabbed the musket into Ruff's wind, the octagonal barrel pushed hard against Justice's suffering body. Iron Heart seemed to enjoy that particular trick a lot.

"Stop that!" she cried.

"Who is he?" Thei asked.

"Ruff Justice. An American."

"What is he doing here, in our hills?"

Toybo pulled on her skirt and blouse. Then she told Ruff's story, slanting it to his best advantage. "He is looking for Sandfire. He was in a fight with the Chiricahuas and was wounded. I am helping him with my medicine. Then he is going to find Sandfire and kill him."

"With what? His bare hands?"

"With a bow and arrow if he has to. Ruff Justice can use all weapons. He has declared war on Sandfire and he will not rest until the butcher is dead. Why are you here?" she demanded abruptly, changing tacks. "What brings you here to disturb me and this American warrior?"

"We are all here. All the people," Thei explained. Toybo's brother examined Ruff with scarcely concealed dislike, but there was some other emotion in his glance as well—interest in what a great American warrior might be like, perhaps. "Get dressed," Thei commanded. Ruff nodded at Iron Heart, who still held the gun on him. Thei spoke sharply, rapidly in the Papago tongue, and the Indian reluctantly withdrew, his dark eyes still watching, his hands still tightly gripping the ancient, deadly weapon.

Ruff dressed slowly, his wounds still demanding caution. The two warriors spoke to Toybo using Spanish instead of their native tongue. The others remained as originally positioned, silent.

"Where did you find this man?" Thei probed.

"You say all of the people are here," Toybo interrupted. "Why?"

"We have no place else to go."

"The high valley . . ."

"Sandfire came. The village was burned. Fortunately we were warned, and we fled before the Apaches came."

"Fled!" she said scornfully. Iron Heart's expression grew angry. Shame lurked beneath the anger, Ruff Justice thought.

"There was no choice. The warriors of Sandfire carry repeating rifles now. New rifles that were supposed to go to the white soldiers, the norteamericanos."

"Where did Sandfire get them?" Ruff interjected. His Spanish was rusty, but he was following the conversation well enough. It occurred to him that perhaps he was supposed to follow it. Maybe that was the reason they spoke Spanish.

"I do not know," Thei replied.

"Stole them?"

"I do not know," Toybo's brother repeated more angrily. "What is it you do?"

"I'm an army scout," Justice said. He tugged on his left boot and stood, fully dressed, watching and waiting.

"American army?" Iron Heart asked.

"That's right."

"From where?" he demanded.

"Fort Bowie."

"Under Major Cavendish?"

"Temporarily, yes. I'm down here to look for Sandfire, but as you must know, we can't chase him into Mexico. There's an agreement between the Mexican government and my own that allows penetration into foreign territory *only* if you're in 'hot pursuit' of Apache raiders. We never found ourselves in that kind of situation. We never got that close to Sandfire, to tell the truth."

"The Papago know him. The Papago can find him. You tell that to your Major Cavendish," Thei said pompously.

Ruff solemnly assured him that he would.

"He has just said the American army will not come after Sandfire," Iron Heart scoffed.

"But they have sent a scout!" Thei looked puzzled. Justice was sent to find the enemy, so that he could be captured, was he not? The warriors looked at Ruff in contemplation.

"He is here for another reason, not to find Sandfire," Iron Heart said with some perception.

"I want Sandfire," Justice said truthfully.

"But you did not come to Sonora to look for him."

"Yes, I did. For him and for another man—a soldier who killed his officer."

"A man with a red beard?" Iron Heart asked with a disdainful shrug.

"Yes! How did you know?"

"I have seen him. I knew he was a criminal. Why else does a lone American soldier ride into the desert? I thought he was a deserter."

"He was alone?"

"Yes."

"When was this?" Ruff asked, growing more interested. Maybe there was still a chance of catching up with Dutch McCoy.

"Two days back. Yes, two days," Iron Heart said.

"Do you know where he is now? Do you know where he was going, Iron Heart?"

"Of course, I know where the red-bearded soldier was going. The Rancho Paseo Prieto. To the rancho of Don Carlos."

8

····◆►•····

Ruff just stood looking at the Papago warrior for a minute, trying to assimilate the information. Everything was tying itself together. He had wondered why Dutch McCoy was beelining it south, as if he knew exactly where to go. McCoy had known.

He was a thief and a murderer, and he had been planning to hold up the army payroll. But had that been his own brainstorm? Or was Dutch being used by a more clever mind? Ruff figured the second possibility was more likely.

Sure, McCoy had known where to go. There was a nest of crime in the mountains of Sonora—Aguilar, who had a snake for a son and a black widow for a daughter, trafficked, Ruff reckoned, in rustled stock, slaves, arms. Where else had the Apaches gotten those repeating rifles Iron Heart had mentioned?

Aguilar, who apparently liked to pose as a Spanish aristocrat, was nothing more than a robber baron, a thief.

Aguilar had very likely given Toybo the bad medicine intentionally. Why, Justice didn't know. Perhaps the Papagos were in his way, perhaps he coveted their high valley, perhaps he had done it to please his savage allies, the Apaches, who were the timeless enemies of the small mountain tribes.

"You are silent. What are you thinking of, escape?" Iron Heart demanded.

"Not of escape, no. I'm thinking that we have to council, that you and I have something in common, Iron Heart, Thei—something that needs thinking out."

"I do not understand you. What could we have in common? What do we need to council about, white scout?"

"Why, war, Iron Heart. You and I have got us a war to make."

Iron Heart didn't react. He stared at Justice as if he were the craziest man of all time. He didn't like Justice. He didn't like Justice sleeping with his woman, even if he himself didn't want her.

Thei was the one who spoke. Toybo's brother moved in front of Iron Heart, removing the threat of that musket for the time being.

"What war do you speak of, Justice? What war could we make together?"

"A war against the Apaches. And against Don Carlos—I think he furnishes them with guns. I think he encourages them."

"You do not *look* as if you can fight. Maybe you were doing what you are best suited for last night," Thei scoffed.

"Maybe. Maybe I'm not ready to fight yet, but I'll heal. I have enough anger in me to make myself heal quickly."

"Anger at Aguilar?" Thei asked.

"Yes, mostly at him."

"Anger is not enough," Thei said.

"No," Justice agreed. "It isn't. That's why we've got to council and decide what we can do."

Iron Heart stepped forward again. "We do not need you, Justice! If we wish to make war, we will make war."

"Like you did when the Apaches pushed you out of the high valley? By fleeing you make war?" Toybo added.

"Shut up. It was not our fault. I told you they had repeating rifles. What are we to do, throw sticks at the Chiricahua?"

"That's something we've got to consider," Justice said.

"What do you mean?"

"I mean we've got to get some better weapons. That musket you've got will kill, but it fires once every two minutes. That's not enough."

"They are all we have," Iron Heart explained.

"We'll get others. Repeating weapons," Justice promised.

"Where? From the Father in Washington? From out of the sky?" Iron Heart demanded facetiously.

"No. We'll get them from the man who seems to have plenty of them—Don Carlos."

"You are mad," Iron Heart said, raising his arms in exasperation.

"Probably. But that's where we'll get them."

"How do you know he has rifles?" Thei asked.

"I'm assuming he's the supplier for Sandfire's men. Why he's doing it, outside of profit, I'm not sure. Maybe he recognizes the obvious fact that there's no real control of Sonora by the Mexican government. We're too far from Mexico City. Maybe he hopes to set himself up as little emperor, the king of the

Apaches. I just don't know. But I do know he wants power and wealth, and he's not going to let anything as minor as a band of Papago Indians stand in his way."

"You talk much. What do you know?" Iron Heart sneered.

Ruff had to admit that the Indian had a point, but he was sure in his own mind—and what he didn't know, he meant to find out. Somehow.

"You must come with us, sister," Thei said, veering away from Justice and his mad ideas of war against the Apaches.

"What do you mean?" Toybo asked, confused.

"The old one, Shamak, is injured."

"How injured?"

"An Apache bullet."

"You said no one was killed or wounded!" There was pain and anger on her face.

"Just the old one. He did not even tell anyone until we were far away from the valley. He fell over and we found the blood on his shirt."

"Who's this 'old one'?" Ruff wanted to know.

"The shaman. Our magic man," Toybo explained hastily. "The one who taught me much about healing."

"He asked for you," Thei said in a way that indicated no other Papago would have asked for Toybo, the witch woman, the healer who killed.

"Where is he? Take me there now," she ordered.

"Our camp is being made in the trees," Thei said, meaning the pine forest below, where the Papagos wouldn't be visible to searching eyes. "They have made him a crude wickiup. He has a fever. There is no chance." Toybo's brother shrugged. "He is old and has lost much blood. Still, it might ease his mind to see you working magic over him."

"And it just might heal him," Toybo said sharply, flaring up.

"You don't have much faith in your sister," Ruff said.

"Faith in a doctor who kills her patients?" Thei said.

"You mean the pox?"

"You have said it."

Ruff told him that he thought Aguilar had given Toybo bad medicine.

The warrior shrugged. "You say much, Ruff Justice. How much can you prove? I know only that Toybo promised to heal the people, and she did not. Not with her herbs and barks and dung, not with the white medicine. Besides, why would Aguilar want to kill us?"

"To get you out of the mountains. You're in his way. You're an enemy of the Apaches, and he sees you as a potential threat. Tell me, does your land surround his rancho?"

"Yes, but . . ." Thei's brow furrowed.

"Let us go," Iron Heart snapped impatiently. "What good is this foolishness? For myself I do not choose to listen to this madman. Ask yourself, Thei, what does *he* want from us?"

"Yes." Thei looked at Ruff thoughtfully and nodded. "You are right, Iron Heart, there is no time for this. Let us see to the old one and then let us organize our forces—without this white man who would be our general."

The Papagos started toward the mouth of the cave, and Justice fell in beside Toybo.

"Where are you going?" Iron Heart demanded.

"With you," Justice said.

"You are not wanted." Iron Heart gave Ruff a little shove with his elbow. He staggered back a step, holding himself in check. The wind, gusting up the canyon, touched them, shifting Justice's long dark hair.

"I think maybe Toybo wants me with her."

Iron Heart wasn't going to budge on this. He had seen and heard all he wanted of Ruff Jusice. He was ready to fight to make sure the American departed one way or the other.

Thei was disgusted. "Come on, Iron Heart. It does not matter."

Iron Heart stared at Justice, his eyes cold. Then he muttered something in the Papago tongue and spun away, walking downslope with his tribesmen.

"What did he say?" Ruff asked Toybo.

"Only that he would kill you."

"Think he'll try it?" Ruff asked, watching the tall warrior go.

"He has said it," was her only answer.

Ruff Justice walked with Toybo through the stand of blue spruce toward the makeshift Papago village that lay where the forest met a rising stone bluff, protecting the rear of the camp from attack. The day was clear, the wind fresh. Jays hopped from bough to bough in the spruce trees, squawking, complaining, bedeviling the gray squirrels that lived there.

They emerged into a small clearing shaded by trees, where twenty or thirty wickiups of branches and brush had been thrown up hurriedly. Hostile, curious, indifferent dark eyes stared at them as they passed, and Ruff wasn't sure if the hatred was for Toybo or for himself.

The first woman they met refused to answer when Toybo asked where the old one, Shamak, was. A boy of ten or twelve pointed farther on, toward the verge of the clearing, where a gray pine stood starkly against the blue-green background of the living trees.

Inside the wickiup it was dark, stale, and silent. The roof was very low. Ruff ducked, following Toybo inside. There was no one tending to the old one, no one keeping watch over his sickbed. It was as if the tribe had abandoned him as well.

There was an unmoving figure on a bed of boughs across the wickiup. At first Ruff thought the old one had died, but as Toybo moved closer, a gnarled hand stretched out toward her, and she took it, dropping to her knees beside the bed and kissing the bony hand.

"Shamak, where is the wound?" Toybo asked the elderly man.

"The belly, Toybo. A bad one, very bad."

"Let us get to it, then, and heal you." She started to rise, but Shamak tugged her down.

"No. It is too late. I know this. I did not send your brother to find you because I wanted medicine, but because I wanted to see you again. It has been so long since these old eyes have seen your happy smile. Since these crazy men forced you from among us . . ." He made a disgusted sound. "Fools. Someone is with you?"

"Yes. An American. Ruff Justice. A friend."

"I am sorry I am not well enough to be hospitable," the old one said.

"But you must let me see your wound," Toybo insisted. She started to pull down his blanket.

"No. It is very bad. The bad spirits have already

entered through the hole and gotten into my blood. The flesh putrefies. It is too late."

Toybo lowered her head and rested her cheek on the medicine man's hand. Justice, feeling out of place, stood motionless in the darkness, watching the life ebb from the old man.

"Damn the Apaches," Toybo said in sudden rage. Then she shook her head, ashamed at the outburst, at having yelled in the sickroom. The old one patted her hand.

"I am sorry," Toybo said. "Forgive me."

"For showing you that you love old Shamak? For revealing to an old man that his life was not useless and that he leaves behind someone who will care enough to nurture his memory?" There was a moment's poignant silence before Shamak added, "Besides, it was not an Apache who shot me, Toybo."

"Thei said the Apaches attacked the high valley camp!"

"Yes, they did. Or they intended to. Our scouts warned us and the people made their escape into the hills. I was foolish and stayed behind. I delayed too long, and when I started up the trail, I was seen by the Apaches. The Apaches and the white men with them."

"The white men!" she cried.

"Yes. There were whites with them. One of these men shot me. One of these has killed me. A white man," Shamak said, "with a big red beard."

"With a red beard?" Justice nearly leapt forward. "A big man?"

"Yes. A big man. He shot me. I dragged myself off and they let me go."

Toybo looked at Ruff Justice. "This Dutch McCoy you have spoken of?"

"I think so. I could be wrong, of course, but how many men with red beards are roaming this desert just now?"

"Why would he be with the Apaches?" Toybo asked.

"Just earning his pay. McCoy is a warrior too."

"You know this man?" Shamak asked from his bed. "This man who has killed me?"

"Yes," Ruff Justice said, "I think so."

Which didn't do Shamak any good. The bad spirits had still invaded his body, and he would die. There was nothing anyone could do about it. Toybo sat holding her mentor's hand while the hours slowly passed. The old man died before the sun had gone down. From time to time he had lifted his head or feebly reached for Toybo. Now and again he had spoken, some of it quite articulate, some of it making no sense at all. Only once in that time did he speak directly to Justice.

He had lifted his head and said quite distinctly, quite dispassionately, "I want you to find this man for me. I want you to find him and kill him, Ruff Justice."

Outside, the sky grew dark and the trees jutted jagged teeth against the sunset. An owl hooted distantly, and Ruff glanced that way. Toybo slipped beside him and took his arm.

"I'm sorry," Justice told her.

"He was a good man."

"He must have been, if you cared for him like that."

"A very good man," she said as if she hadn't heard him. She suddenly squeezed his arm more tightly, turning her eyes up to him. "What are you going to do?"

"About his request? Find the man, of course, and kill him."

"Good." She let out her breath in a tight little hiss. "Let us walk a little way, Ruff Justice," she suggested, "a little way from this place of death."

She kept hold of his arm, and they started through the trees. The air was ripe with their scent. A dog yapped uncertainly somewhere. A woman called for a child.

They wove their way through the trees for silent minutes, then Toybo stopped and turned to Ruff. She clung to him, her arms encircling his neck, her body slacking against his, molding itself to his. He held her, knowing this was a part of her grief.

"I still want to talk to your brother and Iron Heart, the other leaders," Ruff said.

"You still want to make your war?"

"Yes." He kissed the tip of her nose and cupped her breast, holding her nearer.

"You are not well," she said.

"Well enough to fight."

"You speak as if you had an army to take against the Apaches and Don Carlos."

"I do have an army. The Papagos."

"No." She stepped back, looking down at his hand. "They will not fight."

"Why?" he asked.

"We are a small people, and like a small animal, it has always been our way to run."

"The small animal gets devoured, Toybo."

"Only if he tries to fight."

"Is that what you believe?" he asked her, his hands falling away.

"I do not know any longer. I only know they will

not talk to you, fight with you. They are not cowards, but they know they have no chance."

"I see." Ruff nodded, looking at the dark sky above the pines. "Well, then, that's the way it must be."

"What will you do, Ruff Justice? What can you do?"

"Make my own war, Toybo. After all, I made a promise."

"Alone?" she asked, a bit surprised.

"Looks like I'll have to. I'm going to try talking to Thei, but if I have to go alone, I will."

"When?" she asked in sudden panic. "And how?"

"How, I don't know. The best I can, I suppose. When? Well, when I'm healed, half-healed . . . soon."

"But not tonight."

"No, Toybo," he said, drawing her nearer, "not tonight."

"Then there is time to make love."

"There is time," he said, and he kissed her before lying down with her amid the spruce trees.

9

The forest floor was a vast carpet of pine needles. The night was warm and the earth scent was everywhere, the scent of trees, of passing time, and of woman. Ruff Justice kissed the naked Toybo, his mouth finding her throat, her chin, and her soft breasts as his hand nestled between her legs. Stars winked through the tall spruce trees and the wind caused a gentle stirring in the forest. Ruff could feel a different sort of stirring in his groin—a demanding, needful, wanting stirring, and he parted Toybo's legs, feeling her dampness, her own need.

"A minute," Toybo said, and she rolled to her hands and knees, pulling away from Ruff. "Please?" she asked, and she didn't have to ask twice.

As Ruff Justice eased up behind her, she bowed her head, reached back, and placed him inside her, her body thrusting against his, moving and swaying.

Justice rested his hands on her smooth buttocks and ran them down the strong line of her back, leaning far forward to clutch her breasts as she rocked against him with small movements that became shorter and harder as she reached back and cupped

Ruff's sack, holding him against her, her body surrounding his with warmth.

Her cheek was against the pine needles beneath her, her dark hair spread out against the earth. Justice began to pitch and sway against her even harder, driving it in, seeing the expression on her face tense with the pleasure of each long thrust, feeling her fingers stroke him where he entered her, urging him on to a sudden, hard completion that left him trembling against her in the night.

Toybo rolled over, going flat on her back, and pulled Ruff to her, inserting him again. She reached out and found her her skirt, then covered them with it, stroking his back and kissing his throat and chest as he lay there, his body cooling, his pulse slowing.

"Do not go, Ruff Justice," she whispered. "Do not go and make your war. Stay with Toybo."

There was no answer from the night, and she lay back resigned, knowing he would go and make his impossible war.

Thei was standing with a group of warriors when Justice found him early the next morning. They were apparently setting up their sentry posts and schedules, though Justice couldn't follow their language. Thei would point to the high peak or to the stony bluff, and heads would nod. Now and then an armed Papago warrior would take off at a trot to assume a position. Ruff squatted down and plucked a few brown blades of grass while Thei finished.

"What is it?" the Papago war chief asked in Spanish after he was through.

Ruff rose. "I just wanted to talk to you about making a fight of this."

"No. There is to be no fight. The fight is over."

"Have you told the Apaches that?"

"They have no reason to attack us. I do not believe they will follow us."

"And if they do?"

"Then it will be *our* fight, Justice, not yours," Thei said angrily. "Who are you to wander in here and tell us what we must do? Who are you to make yourself leader of the Papagos?"

"Just a man who's seen war, Thei—who's seen it, doesn't much care for it, but believes the best way to come out is as a winner. And the best way to win it is to be ready to fight."

"There will be no war," Thei said stubbornly. His lips barely moved as he spoke. Anger tightened the muscles of his throat and caused his hands to clench. He wasn't very crazy about this American who had come down here, seduced his sister, and was now trying to run things. Justice figured he could understand that, maybe. There wasn't anything left to say, and Ruff turned and strode away. He found Toybo at the forest edge, waiting for him. There was a sack of provisions in her hand.

"What's this?" he asked.

"Our food."

"*Our* food? No, Toybo. Where I walk, I will walk alone."

"You do not know the way," she protested.

"I'll find it. You can describe it. You're not going."

"Why are *you* going?" she asked in frustration.

"What can I do? Stay here, live with you?"

"Yes!"

"No. I came down here to do something, and I

91

mean to do it if I can. That's what they pay me for, and I've been taking their money."

"To kill McCoy?"

"Kill or capture."

"And how will you get back to the border?" she scoffed. There was a bit of despair in the depths of her dark eyes.

"I don't know yet."

"The Apaches are everywhere!"

"That's right. And with any luck I'll spot their main camp. Sandfire is here in Sonora, and I was paid to find him as well. I failed in that job. Maybe if I can spot him, something can be done. If the American cavalry can't come in after him, maybe they can get word to the Mexican army. McCoy and Sandfire— that's two things I have to do, two things they're paying me to do," Ruff said. "I'll find them."

"And Don Carlos?"

"*That*," Justice said a little grimly, "is something I *want* to do." Having said that, he took the sack of provisions from her unprotesting hand. "I'll be going. Thank you for all you've done."

"But you will be back?" She suddenly gripped his arms, and her eyes searched his.

"I'd like to think so," he answered.

"I . . ." She faltered and then shook her head. "I can get a horse for you, and a gun—not the best gun, not the best horse, but something that may help you," she said abruptly. "I can show you where the trails are and where the rancho of Don Carlos lies. I do not know where the Apaches are—except that they are out there, waiting to kill you."

"They won't," Ruff said. "Believe me." He took her

by the shoulders, but she turned and walked away, arms folded. Justice followed.

The horse was behind the wickiup, and it lifted its head alertly at the sound of the two. It was a paint pony, maybe ten years old, with stubby legs and a cast in one eye.

"This the horse?" he asked skeptically.

"It was Shamak's."

Ruff looked it over. It was sound, but beyond that, there wasn't much to say for the shaggy little Indian pony. It didn't matter; he was better mounted than he had been, and he hadn't looked forward to doing what he had to do afoot. The horse was wearing an old Texas rigged saddle, and Justice adjusted the stirrups, tightened the cinches, and tied the provision sack onto the saddle horn as Toybo watched silently. There was a scabbard on the saddle and in it a rifle musket. One shot. That was all he would get at any enemy. There was powder and a half-dozen lead balls, but these didn't reassure Justice much. During the war he had used a musket and both sides, North and South, had killed a lot of men with them, but the day of the musket was long gone.

"It is enough?" Toybo asked.

"It'll have to be." He reached for her, meaning to kiss her, but she pulled away. Ruff winked and swung up onto the horse's back. "Thanks, Toybo."

She had half-turned away, but now she spun back, her hand going to Ruff's thigh, her eyes widening with questions Ruff couldn't answer. He bent and kissed her mouth, tasting the salt of a tear, then he turned the pony's head and rode out through the deep spruce trees, leaving Toybo and the Papago village behind.

The horse moved easily under Ruff as they traveled steadily down a long spruce- and cedar-lined canyon where a quick-running creek made white flourishes against the stones lining the bottom. The horse wasn't much, but it had a smooth gait and, with his wounds, that meant a lot to Ruff.

He was far from healed, but it was time to move and he knew it. His head ached a little as he rode, and the bullet wound in his side itched violently, but there was little pain as long as he didn't move quickly.

And then he was moving quickly.

From the corner of his eye he saw the shadow of movement, saw sunlight on steel, and Ruff threw himself from the saddle as the rifle in the trees exploded, sending a bullet whining past Justice's head and into the forest where it clipped a branch from a spruce tree.

Shamak's paint pony danced away in panic as Ruff Justice hit the ground, jarring his shoulder and filling his torso with searing pain. In his hand was the musket. He had had enough presence of mind to snatch it from the scabbard as he plunged from the horse.

Rolling to one side, he dived for the shelter of a fallen log. He had reached that when a second bullet was fired, this one chipping splinters from the gray and weathered log.

Justice ducked reflexively, then rose up and sighted his own musket on the spot where he had last seen the sniper.

The wind chattered in the trees, the river swept by, hissing and frothing. Justice crouched, unmoving, watching the spruce forest, waiting for the right moment to retaliate.

When the attack finally came, it was from behind. Ruff heard the twig snap under a careless foot, and he rolled onto his back. A rifle bullet thudded into the log where his head had been. Justice started to shoot from the ground and then ceased firing. He would curse himself for it later, but he held his fire as he recognized his assailant.

Iron Heart had thrown away his musket, and with a long-bladed knife in his hand, he hurled himself through the air toward Justice. Ruff struck first.

As Iron Heart's knife flashed in the air, Ruff swung his musket with all his force. The steel muzzle slammed into the Papago's jaw, and he was out cold before he hit the ground.

His left hand had come to rest on Ruff's knee. Moving the hand, Justice rose to his feet and wiped back his long hair. He moved to Iron Heart, took the knife from his hand, and tucked it behind his waistband.

"Dumb bastard," Ruff said to the unconscious man. "If you wanted her so badly why didn't you make an effort to keep her?"

Iron Heart was beyond hearing or answering. Justice shook his head in a mixture of sorrow and disgust and walked off in search of the paint pony, which had run a little way and then stopped to nibble at a patch of grass.

Justice adjusted the cinches and swung aboard. Then he was off again, riding toward the heart of Apache country, toward the Rancho Paseo Prieto.

Within a mile or two, the land began to go dry again. The spruce dwindled, became smaller, and then vanished altogether. The stream lost itself in a deep canyon running toward the distant *playa*. Ruff was riding high desert now, a windswept barren stretch of gray rock, gray sage, and an occasional wind-sheared cedar.

Toybo had given him an idea of how the land lay, but things are never the same as they are in the imagination, and Justice was having some difficulty. He found a trail and began to follow it. The last man to pass this way had known where he was headed, and Ruff meant to follow him.

The tracks were those of a lone Apache, Ruff guessed.

He had been afoot, not unusual for a Chiricahua, as the Apache always did favor fighting on his two feet. His footprints, made by the Apache's unique high boot, were easy to trail. The man had had no fear of being followed by his enemies. But why should he have? No one was there but the Papagos, and they were badly intimidated.

Ruff wondered where the tracks would lead him. But at least the Indian was headed in the same general direction as Justice, and at least *he* knew where he was going. To the Apache camp? It seemed likely. What Ruff couldn't know though, was whether the Indian was one of Sandfire's warriors or a member of another band of Apaches.

"What if it is one of Sandfire's people?" Justice asked himself. Finding the Apache war leader's camp was of infinitely more value than bringing back Dutch McCoy's scalp. The smart thing to do would be to hightail it north, if he succeeded in locating Sandfire.

That was the smart thing.

But what he wanted to do was find Sandfire, skin Dutch McCoy, and deliver a little retribution to the Aguilar clan. Hoping for the three points seemed to be stretching luck a little for a man with a beat-up Indian pony, a wounded body, and a rifle musket.

It was all moot anyway, as he hadn't found anyone, seen a sign of life, smelled smoke, or even heard a horse whicker. There was only the desert, the salt flats below, and the mountains behind him, where a witch woman was busy burying an old friend.

Quite suddenly there was a lot more than that. They seemed to grow up out of the ground, surrounding Justice. He didn't even have time to reach for his musket. But it wouldn't have done him a hell of a lot of good against ten Apaches, anyway.

"Led me right into the trap, didn't he?" Justice asked the horse. "I must be getting old to follow those plain-laid tracks like that."

And the way things looked, he wouldn't be getting much older.

They were all dressed in loose-fitting white shirts, white trousers, and high moccasins. They wore headbands, most of them crimson in color, and they carried spanking new Winchester repeating rifles.

Their leader was a stocky man with one bad eye. He walked to the horse, looked up at Justice, and yanked him from the paint's back. Ruff hit the ground, rolling to avoid the kick aimed at his head. However, it glanced off his skull and left him with a ringing in his ears.

Justice figured a lot worse was yet to come. He tried to get to his feet. He wanted to go out standing at least, not groveling on the ground. He rose, expecting anything: a knife in the gullet, a bullet in the head, a crushing blow from a stone-headed club. But the Indians didn't move.

He stood facing the leader of the Apaches, his chest

rising and falling too rapidly, his blue eyes cold and hard. The Indian gazed at him and nodded. Then he spat out something Ruff didn't understand and Justice was grabbed from behind. Rawhide thongs were looped around his wrists. Ruff struggled briefly, violently, but it was an uneven contest. A rope was thrown around his throat and drawn tight, and Ruff's head was yanked back by an unseen Apache behind him.

They snatched up the reins to the paint pony and started southward, Ruff Justice with them, led by a rope around his neck.

They hadn't killed him, hadn't tortured him—not yet, at least, Ruff thought. Why not? They were taking him captive, but he couldn't imagine what for. He would have thanked his lucky stars for letting him live, but it is said that one is better off dead than a captive of the Apaches.

He didn't know what lay ahead, but he did know that it wasn't going to be pretty. They had plans for him, and Justice would have bet he wasn't going to like those plans one bit. He looked at the silent dark faces around him and trudged on. The day had suddenly turned very cold.

10

··•··──◆──··•··

They reached the Chiricahua rancheria at sunset. Ruff was dog-tired, thirsty, but still reasonably sound. The rancheria, the Apache camp, was situated on a dry, domelike hillock in the shade of a saw-toothed mountain range. Ruff looked around carefully, taking in the landmarks, estimating distances. Not that this information was ever going to be of use to anybody; it was simply habit.

There were a dozen lodges in the camp, most of them thrown together out of brush and bent poles, carelessly made, built to be abandoned. There were no Apache women in the camp—no children, either. It was a war camp.

The prisoners were huddled together beneath a dead, broken cottonwood tree some forty feet high.

An iron ring had been fashioned to girdle the tree, and to it were tied a dozen and a half lengths of rope. The prisoners were mostly young females, a fact that fit with what Ruff Justice had heard about the slavers' patterns. For that was surely what these Apaches were, slave traders.

They must have figured they had some special use

for Ruff, but whatever made him distinctive, Justice had no idea. There was one other mature male there, and he was distinctive. Most distinctive.

Ruff learned his name was Bombo. He was the biggest man Justice had ever seen, bar none. He was an Indian, but from what tribe, Ruff didn't know. His chest seemed to be two feet deep, his shoulders rounded masses of muscle. His face was stolid and blank, oxlike. He looked up without interest as Ruff was tied beside him, pushed to the ground, and left in the dust with the other captives.

A half a dozen Apaches stood guard around them; they must have figured this load was worth watching.

Ruff felt for the young orphaned children, most of them snatched from the arms of dying relatives or tribesmen. They were headed for a life of constant drudgery if not of eternal torment.

There were three or four women who might be considered desirable if they were cleaned up, Justice guessed, but the expressions on their faces, the hang-dog tilt of their heads, the weary hopelessness in their eyes, brought only pity to Justice's thoughts.

"What are they going to do with us?" he asked Bombo. The giant turned empty eyes to Ruff and shrugged massively. He was only a faithful dog, a gentle thing. If the gods had decided to give him to the Apaches, so be it. If they took him to Chihuahua and hitched him to a plow, he would pull that plow. Ruff looked at the others; he would receive no help there. A small boy gazed at him with wide, dark eyes and Ruff smiled. The kid turned away quickly.

Ruff knew he had to get the hell out of there, but how was another matter. He had been stupid enough to blunder into the Apache trap; they weren't going to be stupid enough to let him slip away—not while he was worth money, which apparently he was.

The sky was beginning to go dark. No one came with food; no one asked for any. There was no water. The other prisoners curled up like dogs in a pack, and with nothing else to do, Justice joined them. He lay there, one eye open, watching the guards crouched on their heels, rifles across their knees. He couldn't pick up much of what they said, but heard one word reverently repeated numerous times.

Sandfire.

These were Sandfire's people, then. Ruff had found one of their camps. Great, he thought, it would do the U.S. army a lot of good now. Ruff lay there working at the leather thongs that bound his wrists together. Hour after hour he slowly stretched them, twisting his wrists, rubbing them against each other until just before dawn he thought he could feel some looseness, some chance of slipping from them. His wrists were raw with the effort, and blood trickled down onto his fingers.

Still, there was some looseness, some give. As his eyes lifted to his guards, two of them rose, walked to where he lay, and rolled him over. They had been watching on the sly. They knew.

Ruff's hands were tied again, more tightly this time, and one of the guards kicked him in the ribs for good luck. Ruff lay there gasping, his arms cramped and knotted, his face in the dust.

"They do not like that," Bombo said. "I know."

"And now I know," Ruff replied. He sat up woozily, shaking his head, staring first at the gradual lightening of the eastern sky, and then at the dark figures of the Apache guards standing before the sunrise.

They were up and walking an hour later. Ruff and Bombo were tied together, their hands placed before them and laced to a length of wood like yoked oxen. The women were similarly treated, the children kept on loose lengths of rope. There was a short pause as the Apaches set fire to their camp. Why, Ruff didn't know, but it was obvious that they weren't coming back this way again.

They walked down a long, mustard-colored canyon, while the sun rose and glared down at them. The land was wind-fluted, raw, and jumbled, seemingly untouched by moisture. Here and there a little twisted red manzanita clung to the cliffs, or a Spanish dagger, but that was all. The land could support nothing else. It was a poor land, a harsh land.

At noon the prisoners squatted in the shade cast by the canyon wall that loomed half a mile above them. There the Apaches gave them a gourd of water to pass from hand to hand. The women drank greedily, as the children cried out for the liquid. Bombo looked at the guard disdainfully when it finally reached them. Ruff wasn't so proud. He took two small drinks and handed it back to Bombo, but an Apache guard snatched it from his hand.

"He has had one chance. Maybe he does not need water, this big one," the guard said in Spanish.

Bombo just stared.

A half an hour later they started on again. The canyon seemed endless, and Ruff couldn't pinpoint their location. All he knew was that they were heading east—and down to a lower elevation.

"Look out," Bombo said, yanking Ruff to one side. Three Apache warriors on horses thundered past them up the narrow trail, riding to the head of the column.

Yellow dust sifted down through the air, thick and strangling.

"What the hell's that?" Ruff asked. Everyone looked behind them, expecting what? An army, salvation?

Now the Apache patrol rode past the other way, their numbers swelled by three. Ruff stood next to Bombo, watching.

"Walk on," the Apache in charge of their party called out in three different languages, and the prisoners started onward, their curiosity unsatisfied. Gradually word filtered back from those in the front who had heard the conversation between the Apaches.

The woman in front of Bombo spoke to him rapidly, but softly in a language Ruff didn't know. The giant nodded.

"What was it?" Ruff asked in Spanish.

"Nobody knows. Someone is following, though. They think the Mexican army. The mounted men went back to kill their scouts so they cannot find us."

The information offered a modicum of hope for the more desperate among them—assuming it was true—but Justice wasn't ready to place much faith in the rumor. Nor was he ready to give it up. He was biding his time, recovering his strength, trying to observe the Apaches closely and discover a weakness in their vigilance.

But there didn't seem to be one. He and Bombo, their hands still tied to the length of wood before them, trudged on in silence. Below them a deep, brushy arroyo opened up. If a man could get in there, he could hide like a rabbit, Ruff thought. Maybe the Apaches could get him out, but they'd have to waste a hell of a lot of time. Maybe it just wouldn't be worth it.

But Justice wasn't going anywhere without Bombo, and it wasn't easy to raise enthusiasm in the big man.

"Bombo."

"What?"

"If we could get down into the canyon, we might be able to get away."

"We are tied together."

"We could break out of this once we were down there," Ruff said.

"Then what?"

"You go home," Ruff explained with some frustration. Someone hadn't given Bombo all the equipment he needed upstairs. Maybe it had all gone to muscle.

"Home is a long way, a very long way," Bombo said, and then he refused to talk about it anymore. An hour later it didn't matter. The canyon flattened and widened, becoming a grassy valley opening onto a flatland dotted with other grassy hills. There were some cattle wandering the range, and in the distance stood a vast two-story adobe hacienda with a high wall around it and many trees inside the courtyard. There were half a dozen outbuildings, several of them large enough to house an army platoon.

"What is that?" Ruff Justice wanted to know. "Ask them what this place is called."

The answer filtered back slowly from the prisoners up ahead, from those who knew. "It is a bad place, a very bad place. It is called the Rancho Paseo Prieto."

Justice laughed out loud. He was a hell of a fine tracker. He had set out to find the Apaches, and he had found them in no time at all. Less than twenty-four hours later, he had also found Aguilar's rancho.

"You're so damn smart it hurts," Justice muttered to himself. Bombo looked at him blankly.

They walked on.

Nearer the rancho Ruff could see that the valley was heavily guarded, virtually fortified. Vaqueros armed to the teeth roamed the area on fast horses. Here and there bands of Apache Indians, Chiricahua, and some Mimbres had made their camps. It was getting late, and the fires had been started. Apache kids ran out and amused themselves, throwing rocks at the passing prisoners. One struck Ruff in the back, another in the leg. Bombo was their favorite target, however, because of his size. They tormented him with rocks and sticks, but he ignored it all.

The kids were called back and cuffed, as the prisoners walked nearer to the big house, the hacienda de Don Carlos, the pirate's den.

Ruff could see lights burning behind the barred upper-story windows, above the tall adobe walls that were topped with broken glass embedded in the mortar. Around the house vaqueros stood or squatted, smoking, their faces hidden in the shade of their huge sombreros.

The prisoners were taken to one of the large outbuildings Ruff had seen, a good distance from the house. There were bars on the windows there as well. The buildings were slave quarters, prisons.

The sun was orange behind the huge oaks, the sky deep purple, as they waited to be untied, counted, and taken in. A yellow dog sniffed at Ruff's pantleg, found it uninteresting, and went on.

Bombo yawned. Some of the women cried, while the children sat on the ground, silent and exhausted. They could hear soft voices inside the building, occasionally rising to a fierce curse, subsiding, sobbing quietly.

A vast, mustached Mexican appeared, walking through the Apache guards. He had two rifle-carrying vaqueros with him. The prisoners were examined carefully. A torch was held up, and the women's teeth were checked. Their legs and breasts were felt, their skirts lifted. Children were pinched and poked, prodded and patted.

The Mexican stopped in front of Ruff Justice. He held the torch higher and grinned a gold-toothed grin.

"You have done well, Sagotal," he said to the Apache leader. "You and Sandfire will be rewarded for this."

"Five hundred pesos," the Apache said, and the Mexican turned ugly.

"I said you will be rewarded. The price I do not know."

"Five hundred pesos," Sagotal repeated.

The Mexican ignored him. "Untie this one," he ordered his men.

"Sí, Palermo."

Palermo looked next at Bombo, nodding his approval. "No wonder you kept this one alive—look at those shoulders! He'll work like a mule. The silver mines in Chihuahua will suit him, once he's cut."

"Cut?" Bombo said dully.

"Yes, big one. Takes the fight out of you, leaves the muscle, eh?" Then Palermo moved down the line, leaving Bombo to wonder.

"Cut?" Bombo asked Ruff Justice.

"You know," Ruff said, and he made a gesture that caused Bombo's eyes to light with fury, fear, and panic. He tried to break free, but they clubbed him down, and he fell in a heap as Sagotal's people beat him with rifle stocks.

Justice stood motionless until they cut him free of the rawhide ties. "Where are they taking me?" he asked the vaquero who was overseeing the operation. There was no answer. "If they've got plans to cut me too, tell me now and you can shoot me here."

"*Muy hombre*, eh?" the Mexican asked with a laugh. "Don't want to lose your *huevos*, eh?"

Ruff decided he didn't care a lot for this one. He tried to kick him in his own *huevos*, but the Apache guards held him back. The vaquero laughed.

"It is a good thing they want you, my friend," the Mexican said. "Or I would kill you in a second."

"You wouldn't kill me, friend, if I had a knife, a gun, a club, or a pointed stick. You haven't got what it takes to stand up to a man, *amigo*."

The Mexican, stung, started toward Ruff, but Palermo—who had been watching the byplay with a minimum of interest—barked a terse command.

"Leave him alone, Alejandro. This one is worth money to us."

"He thinks he is much a man ..." Alejandro's heart pumped with anger. He breathed in and out roughly.

Justice watched him, making a mental note of Alejandro's hot temper, of his need to protect his manhood with violence.

Bombo was still moaning, rising slowly to a sitting position, where he remained, holding his head.

"All right, you," Palermo said to Justice, "get going. Those two will escort you."

Ruff didn't have much choice. Between the two armed men, Ruff started off across the dark yard toward the big house beyond, where lights blazed away and someone fooled with a piano. A piano, Ruff thought, five hundred miles from nowhere in the heart of Apache country!

He was ushered in through a tall, narrow iron gate that was hung with some sort of climbing vine and watched over by another Mexican. Inside was a court-yard with flowers flourishing along the borders. Light from the house bled out onto the tiled yard, forming murky rectangles. A fountain splashed ahead some-where. Justice was turned sharply and placed before a door. The guard to his right knocked, and they waited.

When the door finally opened, a tiny wizened In-dian woman bowed and backed away as Justice was pushed forward into the house of Don Carlos. They passed through the kitchen and then through a large pantry filled with sacks of flour, cornmeal, sugar, coffee, and beans. Beyond that stood a heavy oak door near which an iron key hung on the wall. The Mexicans unlocked the door, pushed Ruff inside, and closed the door behind him. He was alone in the darkness.

The guards went away, leather heels clicking on the tile floor. Ruff looked around for a possible way out, but didn't have much luck. There was no win-dow, only the door, and that was three or four inches thick and strapped with iron. Justice tested it any-way, using all the strength in his arms and legs. It didn't give at all.

Ruff heard someone coming, and he stiffened, ready for almost anything. What did they have in mind, anyway? he wondered. Slow torture?

The big door swung open and there she stood, a

vision in white. Dolores Aguilar looked radiantly beautiful, her dress cut low in front to reveal her smooth, youthful cleavage, her long dark hair neatly arranged and decorated with white lace held in place with a Spanish comb. She smiled. "Dinner will be in half an hour. Please make yourself presentable. José here will help you dress. I hope you like pork roast."

And then she was gone, sweeping away up the corridor as two men entered Ruff's cell with clothing, a mirror and razor, well polished boots, and a tin tub.

"Please, señor," the small, unarmed one said, "your bath."

11

Ruff was scrubbed and dressed in a dark, tight-fitting suit. He was shaved and brushed, and there wasn't much he could do but sit scowling through it all. He had no idea what was up, but there was a cold anger building within him—an anger fed by the thought that he was now a slave. A well-dressed slave, and soon to be a well-fed one, but a slave nonetheless.

He knew damn well it was impossible to fight his way out of there, and he tried to calm himself, to quiet the anger. First of all, he had to get out of the cell, get a look around the hacienda, and see if there wasn't some way to slip free ... assuming he was ever out of the sight of armed guards. The one in the doorway of his cell carried a shotgun and watched every small movement Ruff Justice made as the smaller man, José, finished dressing Ruff, buffing his new boots lightly with a soft cloth.

"*Bueno,*" José pronounced, stepping back. He made a sweeping gesture with his arm, apparently proud of his work in transforming a dirty slave into something resembling a Spanish gentleman.

The other guard gestured impatiently with his scattergun. "Come on. Let's go," he barked.

Ruff walked past him, and the gunman backed away, wary of an attempt for his gun. Justice considered it, but he had seen some bad results come of playing with the business end of a shotgun. Besides, there was no way out. He could leave the house, but there were guards outside, plenty of them.

Instead, he walked straight ahead and then turned left where he was told, passing through a small red-carpeted alcove furnished with two heavy chairs, and into a main corridor.

At the end of that was the dining room, where they all sat waiting for their guest while supper was served by silent, white-coated Indians.

At the head of the table was Don Carlos, dabbing his lips with a linen napkin. A glass of pale wine stood near his other hand. He smiled faintly as Justice was brought in at gunpoint.

To his right was Dolores, smiling brightly. She was absolutely beautiful . . . and treacherous. Across from her was Ramón. His expression was hidden, but Ruff could see the tightness in his neck muscles, the firmness of his jaw. Ramón didn't like this idea much. The bearded man at the end of the table could have cared less. He was eating and the rest of the party be damned.

Dutch McCoy didn't look much like a gentleman no matter how he was dressed. His sparse red hair was slicked back, his beard combed, although there was already food in it. McCoy bent low over his plate and wolfed down the food with both hands. He was wearing a dark-green suit and a crooked tie.

The only thing lacking was Sandfire—and a stick

of dynamite. If someone had offered Ruff those two missing ingredients, he could have rid Sonora and the American Southwest of half of their troubles with one big blow.

"Sit down, please," Don Carlos said majestically.

Ruff was given a chair by an Indian. He sat down and stared coldly at his host.

"He looks quite presentable, eh, Dolores?" Don Carlos said. "I see now why you wanted him. McCoy, your beard is in your soup. After we had left you, Dolores pouted for days. She wanted to bring you home, you see?"

"No, I don't see, Aguilar," Justice said. Some of Aguilar's gentility fell away.

"It does not matter. I am surprised you are alive anyway. How did you survive out there?"

"With a little luck." Ruff's voice was deliberately cold. Dolores seemed not to notice, or not to mind.

"I had to offer a reward for you," she said, taking a small bit of meat on a silver fork and placing it on her pink tongue. "I knew Sandfire's people could find you."

"Fine. I'm just not quite sure why you wanted me," Justice said as food was placed before him.

"You are not?" Dolores said, and then she tittered behind her napkin. Her brother looked at her sharply; McCoy kept slurping his soup.

"Anyway," Don Carlos said, "you must admit that this is better than slow death on the desert." His hand gestured, encompassing the entire table. "This sort of slavery must be of some singularity. I suppose you see yourself as a slave?" Ruff didn't answer, and Aguilar finished up with a small shrug. "It is better than being roasted over a slow fire, and I assure you Sandfire's people are capable of that."

A slab of pork roast was set before Justice. He stared at it for a minute, then practical considerations took over and he began to eat slowly. He realized these people knew nothing about him; he was merely a fool who had stopped to help them fight off a few Indians and had then seen too much. They had no idea he was looking for McCoy, for Sandfire, for vengeance. Dolores was cruel, but apparently blind to any ambitiouns but her own. She had her ideas, all right. Ruff could see them in her dark eyes, in the way she fingered her cleavage, toying with the necklace there, teasing Ruff's manhood.

"I seen him before," Dutch McCoy said suddenly. He sat up straight, tossed his napkin aside, reached for a roll, and buttered it. "I seen him before somewhere."

"Could be," Don Carlos said, "and what is the difference?" He couldn't keep all the distaste from his expression as he watched McCoy cram the entire roll in his mouth and chew it like a cow working over its cud. Ruff wondered briefly why Aguilar tolerated a creature like Dutch McCoy.

"Maybe he's a lawman," McCoy suggested, swallowing hard and reaching for his wine to chase the roll down.

"I do not think so," Aguilar said, studying Justice closely. "Do you, Ramón?"

The younger Aguilar just shrugged and refilled his wineglass.

"And what if he is? Is he going to arrest us, do you suppose, McCoy?" Aguilar broke into a laugh. McCoy stared. Dolores still smiled brightly.

"I seen him somewhere," McCoy repeated stubbornly, studying Ruff.

"Where, Justice?" Ramón Aguilar demanded.

"How the hell should I know?" Ruff answered.

"Who are you, anyway?" Ramón probed.

"An army scout."

"Yes?" Don Carlos lifted one eyebrow. "And behind you is an army riding to rescue you?"

"Hardly," Ruff said with a half-smile.

"Why did you come south?"

"I came to look for that bastard," Ruff said, nodding at McCoy, who stiffened. "He shot an army officer and the man died. The army asked me to see if I could find the coward who did it. It looks like I've found him."

"You son of a bitch," McCoy roared as he launched himself across the table, scattering silver and crystal, food and drink. He landed flat on the table, clutching Ruff's shirt front as Justice kicked away and rose to his feet.

"What's the matter, big man, no table manners? Can't beat a man unless you sneak-shoot him in the face," Ruff taunted.

"That's where I seen you! In the cantina."

Four vaqueros appeared out of nowhere. Two of them held Justice while the others dragged a struggling, ranting McCoy off the table. Ramón simmered in silence, Dolores smiled in amusement, and Don Carlos appeared slightly bored, slightly offended. It might have happened every day. Maybe it did.

"Dutch," Aguilar said as the thrashing badman was lifted to his feet, "that is enough."

"You heard him . . ."

"That is enough," Aguilar repeated, his voice even

softer, even more rich with implicit menace. It got through to McCoy, and Justice saw him relax slightly in the arms of his warders. After another minute, thick chest heaving with residual anger, McCoy shrugged off his keepers and slicked back his hair. He didn't say another word to Justice, but spun on his heel and marched off in a way that conveyed a threat.

Don Carlos laughed. "I think it is a good thing I do not allow weapons at the supper table."

Justice just stared. All a good joke, was it? There was a lot of entertainment to be had at the Rancho Paseo Prieto. He took a slow, deep breath and seated himself at the table once again, but he didn't eat. His stomach had become his conscience.

"Make a lot of money here, do you?" Justice asked.

Don Carlos looked surprised. "Why, of course," he replied.

"There's a profit in human misery, I suppose."

"A *padre*. Ruff Justice is a psalm sayer," Aguilar said, sipping from yet another glass of white wine.

"Hardly," Justice responded. "I've never been accused of being a holy man before. But you don't have to be a *padre* to dislike human hurt, do you?"

"Be sensible, Justice," Don Carlos said. "Look at the desert, at the Apache. Before I came, he was dealing with slaves. He was torturing people, killing them out of hand, entire peoples! But he still lived like a coyote on the desert. He was poor, his enemies were suffering."

"And you came and fixed it all up."

"I came and organized matters, yes. The Apache still raids, but now he is paid for it. Slaves are still taken, but for the most part they are not abused. The mountain tribes are still involved in conflict with the Apaches, but I do not allow Sandfire to slaughter them indiscriminately."

"Not só long as they're breeding slaves," Ruff said bitterly.

Don Carlos chuckled, but there was no humor in it. "You are perceptive."

"But foolish," Ramón put in. He slammed his glass down on the table. "Why do we have to listen to this army scout with his sobbing heart? It's bad enough that we have to suffer the boor McCoy without putting up with this," he complained.

"We put up with him because he is amusing, because your sister wants him," Don Carlos said.

"And so we have to stand his insults?"

"You have always brought your Indian women into this house, Ramón," Dolores said. "So what if I wish to bring this one to me? One man compared to the many women you have brought to your bed."

"I hope he meets the same end," Ramón mumbled, and Ruff began to wonder what sort of family this was, what sort of bizarre ideas they could come up with in the dark of night.

"Nothing will happen to him," Dolores said with finality. "He is my man, my toy, my companion."

"Watch him closely," her brother said, and then he rose, his heavy wooden chair scraping against the floor. Dolores watched him go. Don Carlos ignored his son's departure.

A half-hour followed when no one spoke, when the only sound was that of Don Carlos sipping his wine, of the white-coated waiters whisking away silver and cold food. Ruff spent the time watching Dolores, amazed at her cold dark eyes, the marble and ebony beauty of her, the callousness and brutally frank sexuality.

She didn't know what giving herself honestly to a man could be like, that joy shared was doubled pleasure. She thought only of herself. She would never have understood someone like Toybo, would likely have scoffed at her.

Dolores had bought herself a man, paid for him, and no doubt expected a decent performance. She couldn't have comprehended the revulsion Ruff felt at the sight of this beautiful, remarkably constructed female.

Dinner ended abruptly. Don Carlos rose and patted his lips once again with his napkin. "I am weary. I bid you good night, Ruff Justice."

And then he was gone, followed from the room by two vaqueros, and only Ruff was left, Ruff and the woman who watched him, her eyes bright with want, her nostrils flaring, her breasts rising and falling with need.

"It is time for bed, it seems," Dolores said, her voice raspy and choked with excitement.

"Fine. Where do I sleep?" he asked innocently.

"Where do you want to?"

"Where it's warm and dry and quiet."

"I know a place where it is warm at least." She smiled seductively at him.

"Fine. Have you got a place for yourself?"

Dolores stiffened. "Do you not know what I am offering you?"

"Sure. Slavery."

"I could—" she sputtered.

"What? Kill me?"

"Do you not see what I am offering, what I have to give?"

"Yes. You're going to do for me like your father does for the Indians, Mexicans, and border Americans. You're going to organize things, make it all better for us, make our lives better if it kills us."

She glared at Ruff for a long while, saying nothing; then she rose and walked around the table, her hips moving with feline grace, her entire body sensuous and alive, advertising desire.

"Do you not want me?" she asked. She came to him, halted a foot from him, bent forward, and rested a hand on his knee.

"Sure."

"Really?" It seemed to delight her, as if half the men in the world wouldn't want the beautiful Dolores Aguilar.

"Yes," he admitted coldly.

"I see—but you do not like the woman to push too much, to be in control?"

"That's right," Justice agreed.

"A man in the Spanish style, eh?" She laughed, and as she threw back her head, her white teeth, straight and even, glistened against the pink of her mouth.

"That's right," he replied.

"Liar." She bent her head and kissed him passionately and provocatively. Her breath misted wine; her body was perfumed and powdered, with only a slight scent of woman, woman needful and preying.

"Let's go to bed," Justice said. He held her arm at the elbow and squeezed it until the flesh around his fingers turned white.

"One kiss changes your mind?" she purred.

"That one did."

She laughed again and Ruff wondered if she was

mad or only twisted in her sexuality. Her hand dropped to his crotch and found his manhood. She breathed in sharply, taking his hand. "Come, then."

"You're not mad any longer?" he asked.

"No, not mad. Come on. Now, please."

Ruff rose, and she led him toward a stairway at the back of the room. A guard followed them, a narrow, smirking man with scars around his eyes and a rifle in his hands.

"Is he going to bed with us?" Ruff asked, nodding toward the guard.

Dolores laughed. "No. Go away, Miguel."

But Miguel didn't move. He had his orders from the *patrón*.

Upstairs Ruff found Dolores' room bathed in candlelight, the bed covered in white satin sheets and pillows. The door to the balcony was open and a light breeze blew gently through the curtains, bringing the scent of perfume and powder to Ruff's nostrils.

The door to the hallway still stood open, and Miguel stared into the room with an evil little light in his eyes as Ruff followed Dolores to the bed and watched her unpin her hair.

Looking up, Dolores walked back to the door and kicked it shut in the guard's face.

"Do not lock the door," Miguel said almost pleadingly. "Please, señorita—the don's orders."

Dolores wasn't interested in locking the door. She apparently didn't care whether or not it was locked. She was interested only in Justice. She walked toward him, hips moving gently from side to side, her long, loose hair tumbling down across her shoulders. Her fingers were at the nape of her neck, undoing the snap of her dress. Moments later, her clothing fell to the floor.

"Lie down, Ruff Justice," she ordered. It was a royal command. "Take off your clothes and lie down on my bed."

12

She was beautiful, but oh so cold, a black widow, a preying thing. Her dark eyes sparkling, her lush body provocatively posed at the foot of the bed, Dolores repeated her command.

"Undress, Ruff Justice. I will make love to you like you have never had it before. I am hungry for you, Justice, do you understand?"

Ruff understood well enough. She was lovely and available, and a part of him found her almost irresistibly seductive. But then there was another part of him that sat back and calculated the situation, knowing she was a spidery thing—and like a black widow, when she had sucked him dry, she would devour him.

Her hand reached out, stroked his head, and she drew him to her.

Ruff turned the woman and brought her arm up sharply behind her, placing her fisted hand between her shoulder blades. She tried to cry out, but Ruff clamped his hand over her mouth. She tried to bite him, tried to twist free, but neither worked.

Looking toward the door, Justice dragged Dolores

in that direction. Standing against the wall beside the exit, he removed his hand long enough for her to shriek a brief curse. The door swung open and the guard came in. Ruff grabbed Miguel's rifle by the muzzle, yanked him into the room, and kicked the door shut behind him.

Miguel started to cry out, but Justice's booted foot came up hard between his legs, causing the Mexican's shout to die into a whimpering moan as he collapsed to the carpet. Ruff wrested the rifle from Miguel's hands and turned, grabbing Dolores by the hair as she bolted for the door, clawing at the ornate brass handle.

"Let me go, *cabrón!* Pig bastard!"

"Shut up or I'll let you kiss the butt of this rifle."

"You are not a man, you are *nothing.*"

"That's right," Ruff agreed. "Nothing at all." He looked out into the hallway, his arm crooked around Dolores' throat. There was no one coming; apparently no one had heard.

Ruff closed the door and released Dolores. Miguel was still on the floor, clutching his manhood, his face twisted and pale.

"Give me some of your stockings," Justice ordered the woman.

"What for?" she cried.

"Do it!"

She stalked to her bureau and tore a dozen silk stockings from it, throwing them in Justice's direction. He snatched one up and stuffed it into Miguel's mouth.

"Now tie him, hands behind his back," he commanded.

"Tie him! Me!"

"Sure. We'll leave him in the closet. Maybe later—if you leave him tied—you can force *him* to make love to you."

She let out a string of curses in Spanish. Her hands curved themselves into talons and she raked her fingernails across Ruff's face. He slapped her aside and she sat down hard, staring in silent astonishment.

"Tie him up, I said."

"You will die for this," Dolores hissed.

"Likely." Ruff watched the door, worried more about interruptions than about her automatic threats.

"I will see that you are given to the Apaches. They will know what to do. I will stand and watch them as they cut you and burn you—"

"Tie him and shut up."

She obeyed, binding the guard with pretty blue and red silk stockings. When she was through, they dragged Miguel into the closet and shut the door behind him.

"Now go!" Dolores spat.

"Now *we* go," Ruff corrected.

"We! I go nowhere with you."

"Don't bet on it. There's only one way out for me, and that's with a hostage."

"There is *no* way out."

That was very likely, but Justice was going to have his try. As long as he could keep hold of Dolores, the Apaches and Aguilar's vaqueros would have to keep their distance. Maybe.

Unless Aguilar was as cold as the daughter he had spawned. Maybe he didn't care if his daughter got it or not. But Aguilar had to know he had a lot to lose if Justice got away.

Because if Ruff could make it to the border, he was

going to return—with the cavalry, with the law, Mexican law and American law. McCoy would hang, Aguilar would hang, Sandfire would hang—and most likely a lot of others like Sagotal and Palermo.

He pulled Dolores to him again, holding her arm tightly. The rifle in his free hand was cocked.

"We're going out," he told her. "Out of the house and then to the first two horses we come to."

"And then?" she panted. There was still a wild excitement in her eyes, not all of it fear.

"To the border."

"Impossible."

"We'll see. It's my only chance, remember. If I stay here, I die. So don't do anything to ruin my last chance, do you understand?"

She laughed. Incredibly, she laughed. "Or what? I know you and your kind—you would not kill me. You are soft, Justice. A lot of man, yes, but not hard, not so hard you would kill a woman. You have never done that, you never would, would you?"

"I don't know. There's always a first time. Let's not put it to the test."

Then he walked out into the hall and pulled her after him, his left arm around her, his hand filled with the fabric of her dress. His right hand held Miguel's Winchester at waist level. The corridor was empty, silent. It dawned on Ruff that something wasn't right. Someone should have been around—Don Carlos, Ramón, another guard.

"Easy now," Justice said as they started down the stairs. "Move slowly, quietly."

"Fool! Do you know what you are giving up?"

Ruff didn't answer. He could see the candlelight in the dining room now, but there didn't seem to be

124

anyone in there, either. Somewhere down the hallway a board creaked and Justice froze, peering down.
Nothing. There was no one there. He started on again,
giving Dolores a warning squeeze.

They were five steps from the bottom when the
gunman popped up from beneath the stairwell.

"Señorita Aguilar!" he shouted, and Dolores leapt
for the banister, her dress tearing as she went over
the rail, leaving Ruff with a handful of material.

The vaquero opened up with his pistol, stabbing
flame toward Justice, who answered with an authoritative, single syllable from the rifle. The pistol shots
sprayed all over Hades, knocking plaster loose, shattering the frame of a picture behind Ruff. Justice's
single shot had been delivered with more delibera-
tion. It hit the vaquero in the center of the chest and
slammed him backward into a table that fell as the
gunman, blood staining his shirtfront, died on the
hallway floor.

Ruff vaulted the rail, his hair flying, rifle held
high. Dolores was gone. He caught a glimpse of her
turning a corner and slamming the door, and that
was that. From the other end of the candlelit corridor the thudding of boots sounded and Ruff Justice
muttered a curse. He had screwed this all up.

Going to one knee, he waited until the Mexicans
rounded the corner, then he methodically placed four
.44s into the heart of the mob. Two men went down;
the rest beat a hasty, noisy retreat. Justice made for
the back of the house.

He found the kitchen and rushed through it. Three
old Indians were scrubbing the dishes in a vast zinc
tub, and they turned to gawk as Ruff bolted through
the back door.

He rolled as he went out and it was a good thing that he did. Rifle fire peppered the ground around him, lead whining off the tile slabs as noise and flame filled the courtyard.

Justice never stopped moving. He was in a desperate situation and he knew it—movement was his only hope for survival.

He leapt a low hedge, heard a bullet clip brush beside him, and hurried on into the shadows. A man, holding up a candelabra, appeared at an upstairs window. Don Carlos. Ruff paused in flight long enough to whirl, aim, and send a bullet flying toward the rectangle of light above.

The bullet struck metal and Don Carlos cried out. Ruff cursed. He had gotten only the candleholder when what he wanted to tag was flesh and black heart. Ruff ducked under a low branch and then half-stumbled into a waiting man. The vaquero didn't have a lot of nerve; he seemed to have been crouching there, hoping the battle wouldn't come to him, but it had.

Now in panic the man tried to shove a Colt revolver into Justice's face and trigger off. But Ruff moved first, pushing his Winchester in the vaquero's belly. The force of the slug leaping from the muzzle slammed the vaquero into the rose bushes behind him, where he hung, slowly bleeding to death.

Shots from behind sang past Ruff's ears. There was an adobe wall immediately before him, and bullets ricocheted off it, whining into the night. There was much shouting and torchlight as the pursuit gained momentum, force, and purpose. Ruff looked at the wall, threw his rifle up and over, and then leapt for the top.

His hands were sliced by the broken glass embedded in the wall, and he stifled a cry of pain. Dragging himself over, he felt his knees and thighs torn by the glass as his pants were ripped open.

Standing on the wall, Ruff avoided the bullets that buzzed angrily past his head. Finally, he leapt for the darkness below.

He hit the ground hard, and looking back toward the top of the wall, he searched desperately for the rifle. Luckily he found it just as the first vaquero surmounted the wall, and Justice levered through two rounds, the second bullet tagging the bandit in the face, hurling him back amid cries from those who had been urging him on from below. Justice took to his heels.

Ahead of him loomed the figure of a horse outlined against the starry sky. Beyond the horse was the oak grove, behind it the slave quarters—and more men rushing toward him. Everything was blocked out momentarily as Justice focused only on the horse.

Was it fast, fast enough? Ruff wondered. It was at least a chance. Justice hit the saddle and heeled the startled horse into motion before he'd even grabbed the reins. Now he found them, and holding them with one hand, he fired into the body of men that appeared from behind the trees before him.

He saw the bright, unwinking moon, the far mountains where Toybo worked her magic, the white of the distant *playa*, all at once, as if his eyes could see everything near and far, as if there were no secrets from him on this night. His senses were battle-sharpened, inspired by the excitement that tingled through his body. Justice ducked low behind the stolen horse and fired beneath its neck as he ran a gauntlet of *bandidos*.

Ahead, six mounted men suddenly appeared and Ruff yanked the horse's head to one side, kneeing the animal and slapping it with the rifle butt as he raced to the right past an empty barn and scattered ricks of hay. A rifle barked near at hand and Justice felt the horse stagger. It threw its head sideways and whinnied wildly, showing Ruff a startled white eye. Blood ran darkly from a wound in its neck.

If it could hold on for a little while longer, for another half-mile . . . Behind Ruff the men on horseback opened up and he ducked across the wounded horse's withers once again. He could feel the animal's strength flagging stride by stride.

The split-rail fence appeared out of the darkness across Ruff's path and he knew the horse wasn't going to jump it. The animal hit the fence with its chest, folded up, and rolled. Justice leapt free, or tried to, but the thrashing horse struck him wildly with a foreleg and knocked him down.

Groggily Justice rose and started running, still holding the rifle, which, he realized, must be getting low on ammunition even if it had been fully loaded—and there was no guarantee of that.

The hunters found the horse. Torches wove across the field. Ruff dived for the haystack to his left as three horsemen thundered past the barn and toward the broken fence. There was much shouting behind him. He burrowed into the hay and lay still, heart hammering, hoping for the best.

They had already found his tracks, and he swallowed a curse and watched as an Indian tracker followed them by torchlight. Ruff sighted on his chest and fired, bursting from the haystack as the Indian was thrown back. The guns of the vaqueros opened up.

Ruff ran for the trees beyond the barn and leapt into a gulley, tripping and stumbling, going down hard over exposed tree roots. He ran southward, the moon peering into the gulley at him, the stars winking furiously, the frogs falling silent as he passed.

He took a chance, knowing the gulley was leading him in the wrong direction, away from the border, and he veered right, scrambling up the bank toward a stand of cottonwoods whose heads he had spotted from below. He glanced across his shoulder, searching for pursuit. There was none. The lights in the hacienda seemed as distant as the stars. Ruff was breathing raggedly, but his spirits rose slightly as he reached the cottonwoods and halted abruptly.

They were there, four of them. He brought his rifle up and fired, but it clicked on an empty breech. The click seemed to be a portent of Ruff's own death. The man in the middle was Ramón, and even by the pale moonlight, Justice could see his cruel little eyes light up with glee, see the narrow mouth twist into something resembling a smile.

If his look was dirty and spiteful, the expression on the face of the man next to him was absolutely joyful. Dutch McCoy swung down and walked to Justice.

"You long-haired bastard, I'll have you now . . ."

He reached for Justice, but Ruff swung the rifle, slapping McCoy on the side of the head with it. McCoy went down in a heap. Ruff's eyes flickered to Ramón. The smile was still there, just as nasty. The rifle in Ramón Aguilar's hands, Justice would have bet, was fully loaded. On the ground McCoy stirred and groaned.

"Put the rifle down, Justice," Ramón said.

"Sure," he said, obeying Ramón's command.

"Palermo"—the order came in rapid Spanish—"tie his hands and give me the end of the lariat."

Palermo swung down and tied Ruff, who just stood watching Ramón. There wasn't much point in trying anything else.

"Here, Señor Aguilar," Palermo said, handing the end of the rope to Ramón. Ruff felt a cold chill creep up his spine, a movement like a ball of worms in the pit of his stomach—he knew what was coming, knew it wouldn't be pretty.

Incredibly, Ramón was still smiling when he slapped his big Spanish spurs to the flanks of his horse. The animal leapt into motion and Ruff was yanked forward and thrown to the ground.

Ramón yelled out something Ruff didn't get, didn't pay attention to. The rope was taut around his chest, and the horse was running flat out across the valley.

Ruff hit a rock, felt white-hot pain flame through his brain. He was lifted into the air and dropped again, his body tumbling and twisting, stirring up a cyclone of dust. Behind him vaqueros rode, shooting their guns into the air in celebration. But they were distant memories, dreamlike figures, dark devils.

Only the pain was real. Ruff hit another unseen rock, and the breath was slammed from his body. He felt as if a mule had kicked him in the ribs, the hoof stomping lungs and heart. He was still spinning; Ramón was still shouting. Ruff tried grabbing the rope, tried coming to his feet, but there was no hope of that. The horse was running dead out toward the hacienda beyond the trees. Ruff could see the lights of the house, the trees, the pale moon, but none of it had much meaning.

His coat, ripped and dusty, was in rags now; his pants had no knees. The skin was torn from his knee-caps, elbows, and the palms of his hands. Still, Ramón rode on with Ruff Justice whipping from side to side on the end of the rope.

They rode right into the courtyard of the big house and with much noise—shouting, firing of weapons, Ramón and the vaqueros stopped. Ruff Justice lay still against the earth.

He was breathing in and out, he thought—it was difficult to be sure. He could see Ramón sitting on his horse, could see the squat, broad-faced Indian walking toward him. Then the woman was there, barely dressed, smelling sweet, her body soft and inviting. She crouched down and looked at Ruff Justice. Rising, Dolores Aguilar said coldly, "He's still alive. Take him out somewhere and finish the job."

13

Dolores stood, hell fire in her eyes, savage fury in her voice. She stood and waited, trembling, while Ruff was cut free and lifted to his feet.

"Kill him," she hissed again.

Ramón laughed.

Justice couldn't stand alone, and two vaqueros held him upright, their grips angry—he had killed some of their friends.

"Sandfire," Ramón said to the short Apache Ruff had seen. "He is yours, do what you want. Just make it slow and painful."

The Apache only nodded. He lifted Ruff's head and Justice found himself looking into the coldest eyes he had ever seen: utterly inhuman, without a light of compassion or concern.

"I will make it slow," Sandfire agreed.

"What the hell is going on? Have they got him?" Don Carlos pushed through the crowd. On his heels was Alejandro, wearing jeans, cotton shirt, and a wide brimmed hat, and carrying a rifle. Don Carlos was also in traveling clothes, Justice noted indifferently. He was more concerned with his own hide just then. He was in much pain, but as bad as it was, Ruff knew it could get a hell of a lot worse.

He had found Apache victims before, staked to the ground faceup, their lids cut off so that the sun burned out their eyes. Or with their bellies ripped open, their innards filled with fire-heated stones. They had all sorts of variations: all of them were very ugly, very slow, very painful.

"Damn you, Justice!" Don Carlos stepped to him and slapped him full across the face. Ruff hardly noticed the additional pain. Don Carlos was furious. There was a toughness to his face that Ruff hadn't noticed there before. "You caused enough hell on this night."

"He will not be causing any more," Ramón promised.

"No. He will not." Don Carlos looked at his Apache ally. "What are you doing here? Have you forgotten that we leave at midnight?"

"I have forgotten nothing," Sandfire said sullenly.

"He is going to take care of Justice first," Ramón said happily.

"To hell with that. Shoot him—no, forget that. Palermo, take him to the slave quarters and lock him up. Why waste human flesh?"

"I want him dead!" Dolores spat.

"He is worth money in Chihuahua, *hija*," Don Carlos said. "We will sell him at the mines. You want a slow death for Ruff Justice? There is nothing slower than working your life away in the dust and darkness of a silver mine—I know. It is I who replace the dead with the living. Go now, Sandfire, prepare your people. North in one hour."

The Apache bowed away, his face cunning and arrogant.

Dolores stepped forward to argue. "I want to see him tortured . . ." Don Carlos viciously backhanded her across the face.

"Go to your room and dress. Find some vaquero to cool your sick need. Ramón, change your clothing. Then we go."

They half-led, half-dragged Justice away into the darkness. His last recollection was of Dolores standing there half-dressed, blood trickling from the corner of her mouth, looking at him like some hardened she-wolf.

His body was a mass of bruises, afire with pain. When they reached the prisoners' barracks and then proceeded to pass it, Ruff thought, Uh-oh, this is it. They've decided to take care of me themselves.

But there was a small adobe blockhouse behind the barracks with a guard standing sentry before a heavy door. A single high window, dark now, stared out blankly at the moonlit valley.

"Another one," Palermo told the guard.

The vaquero looked Ruff over, nodded, and unlocked the big door, which squealed on iron hinges. Ruff was thrown inside, and he landed against the floor and lay there, panting, his body aching from head to foot. A hand clutched his shoulder and rolled him over, and Ruff looked up into a familiar face.

"Bombo," he said weakly.

"Yes. What happened to you?"

"I tried to run and they didn't like it." Justice tried sitting up, but he didn't have any success until Bombo put a hand behind him and lifted him. Ruff sat there shaking his head, breathing in slowly, and fingering his aching ribs to determine if they were broken.

"What did they bring you over here for, Bombo?"

"I tried to run too. They hit me."

"Maximum security, huh? What happens now?"

"They cut us," the big man said dully. "Then they take us to Chihuahua to work in the silver mines."

"To hell with that," Justice said, rising to his feet to stand wobbly-kneed in the patch of moonlight that filtered through the high window and stained the floor of the cell.

"What else can we do?" Bombo asked innocently.

"Get the hell out of here, that's what."

"There is no chance of that. They have too many men, Justice."

"After a while they'll have a lot fewer. They're riding north for some reason or another—Aguilar, Ramón, Sandfire, McCoy, and the vaqueros."

"All of them will not go," Bombo said morosely.

"No, not all of them. They'll have to have people guard the slaves and watch the house, but the odds will be some better."

"One man with a gun is too much for us, Justice," Bombo insisted.

"You could be right."

"Then, why try?" the big man asked, his spirit broken.

"Bombo"—Justice put a hand on the massive shoulder—"are you seriously suggesting that we just sit back and let them do what they mean to do to us, sell us into slavery over in Chihuahua?"

"Maybe the soldiers will come," the giant said hopefully.

"And maybe it'll rain silver dollars tomorrow."

"What?"

"Never mind. Look, I'm going to try it. I don't know how, but after midnight when Don Carlos has

135

pulled out, I'm going to try getting out of this lousy adobe box. Are you going to try it with me?"

"If there was a way—but there is no way." He shook his head heavily. Bombo was big and he was strong as an ox, but he didn't have a lot of determination.

Ruff tried egging him on. "Are you sure they haven't already cut you, Bombo?" he asked.

"What do you mean?" Bombo stepped back, his face clouding.

"I mean, are you sure you're still a man? What kind of man sits on his haunches waiting to be killed, to be sold as a slave, to be mutilated?"

"There is no way. I told you: if there were a way, I would break that door down."

"Well, we can try."

"It is no use. Even if I could do it, a man outside would shoot me down. If I live, I have a chance. The soldiers may come."

He said that last bit with a wavering voice; his belief in that fairy tale was waning a little. Still Bombo was adamant. He wasn't going to break out with Justice, or even attempt it.

Well, maybe Bombo was right, Ruff thought, maybe there was no way out. Justice sat glowering, staring at the dark, heavy door of the adobe hut. Something scuttled away in the darkness; the moon shifted its pattern as a cloud drifted across its face. An hour passed. They heard Aguilar and his small army ride out, smelled the dust in the air for a long while afterward.

Bombo had seated himself in the corner to scowl and sulk. Justice moved silently but restlessly around the small room, trying to come up with an idea, trying to measure things.

Was the guard awake and alert? He hadn't heard him moving for some time. Those wood poles set into the adobe that acted as bars across the high window, were they as sturdy as they looked, or possibly rotten? A quick test gave Ruff the answer: they were as thick as Justice's wrists and considerably stronger.

He strained and struggled against them for a long while, gaining nothing but sore shoulders and raw fingers. Bombo sat staring.

"Try them, Bombo. Try ripping these poles out."

"Why? A man comes with a gun and kills me for it."

"He might not hear."

Bombo shook his head and went back to his scowling and sulking. Justice moved to the door, examining the hinges, which were on the inside. But they had been flared over with a blacksmith's art so that they couldn't be driven out, even if a man had a hammer and punch. Ruff had neither. The wood was solid oak. Outside, the guard moved and yawned, then he muttered something—he was awake, all right. Justice cursed softly, profusely.

He searched the interior of the room while Bombo watched with unhappy, black eyes. Maybe if he had a stick, a rock—but there wasn't a damn thing around.

"Sleep," Bombo said. "Tomorrow we will walk a long way. You will need sleep."

Justice didn't answer. The moon was nearly down, judging from the pale light it cast high on the wall. Dawn wasn't that far off. Justice had paced and worried the night away, accomplishing nothing. Maybe Bombo was right, but damn it, he wasn't built the same as the Indian, built to accept whatever came his way. He would struggle and fight and try to mold the world his way—he was bound to fail much of the time, but that wasn't a reason for giving up and going along with whatever the bastards in power, men like Don Carlos, came up with.

The pistol fell through the window and lay against the floor like a darkly gleaming promise. For a moment Ruff was too stunned to move toward it. Then he did, quickly snatching it up before chinning himself on the poles to look out the window. There was no one there, nothing but the dark oaks.

Bombo was beside him. "A gun. Loaded?"

Ruff flipped the loading gate open and turned the cylinder. It was loaded. He snapped the gate shut and stood staring at the window.

"Who?" Bombo asked.

"I don't know. I only hope it's not a trick."

"What kind of trick could it be?"

At least one kind came to mind. There was a woman out there who had wanted Ruff dead, preferably by torture. Her father had locked him up instead. Maybe Dolores wanted him to try to escape; maybe she was out there in the oaks, a rifle stock nudged against her pretty cheek, her beautiful dark eye squinting down the sights, waiting.

"What do we do?" Bombo asked.

"You do what you want. I'm going."

Bombo looked at the gun again, at the big door, at the window where the last of the moonlight shone dully. Then he nodded. "I will come with you," he said. "What do I do?"

"The door. Can you break it down?"

"The door is very solid," the giant replied. "The window . . ."

"You'd never squeeze out the window, Bombo. "It's the door we want."

It was a long time before Bombo finally sighed in agreement. "All right."

Justice slapped him on the shoulder, checked the revolver once more, and positioned himself beside the door. It had to be fast and certain. There was no guarantee that it was going to work, but there was a chance—and come morning, there would be no more chances. They would be yoked like oxen again and marched over the mountains to live out their days in chains. Compared to that, sudden death sounded fine to Ruff Justice.

Ruff had been listening, and he no longer heard the guard stirring. Maybe he had fallen asleep. He couldn't have been anticipating trouble. Many prisoners must have been held in the adobe hut, and none of them had gotten away—yet.

Ruff nodded at Bombo.

The big man crouched and then hurled himself at the heavy door. It had to go the first time, and it did. Bombo went through, the planking splintering as his huge body hit it, and he crashed to the earth outside. Ruff Justice was on his heels, leaping through the door to land crouched, ready. The guard had been sleeping, but now he jumped to his feet, terrified out of a dream. He brought his Winchester repeater up, and Ruff slammed the barrel of the Colt against his face, shattering his cheekbone and sending him back into the depths of his dream. Justice snatched up the rifle, tossed it to Bombo, who was rising groggily, and started around the corner of the adobe, heading for the shelter of the oaks in case the racket had roused other guards.

Ruff stepped around the corner and came face to face with a vaquero with a leveled pistol. Justice, caught in an awkward half-stride, could only lower his head and keep on going. He hit the vaquero in the chest with his shoulder, and they both went down in a heap. The vaquero's pistol exploded across Ruff's shoulder. That would bring them running, Ruff thought, but he didn't have time to worry about the others. This one had him wrapped up well enough.

He tried to knee Ruff, missed, and barely avoided the down-slashing barrel of Justice's Colt. Ruff kicked free, rolled to his feet, and prepared himself to shoot— and to be shot, bracing himself for the impact of lead. But none came. The vaquero went down with a sigh, his eyes blank. Behind him stood Toybo with a musket held like a club in her hands.

"Toybo!" Ruff cried thankfully.

"It is I. We must run."

"Wait, my friend." Justice grabbed her hand and held her until a panting, stumbling Bombo caught up. Then they all ran for the oaks. From the house they heard shouts as other guards, summoned by the shot, made for the adobe.

"What are you doing here?" Ruff asked as they ran.

"What do you think? I followed you."

"Why?"

"*Why*? Crazy man, you do not know why?"

"I'm glad you did, Toybo." They ducked under an oak limb and ran on. "I don't know if we've gained much, though. I don't see how we're going to make it."

"I have horses," Toybo announced proudly.

"Three?"

"Two. I did not know you had a friend."

"All right. Where are they?"

But finding the horses proved to be more difficult than expected, as they weren't where Toybo had left them. When the three reached the spot five minutes later, breathless and weary, Toybo could only stand and stare, looking into the shadows.

"Where are they, Toybo? Damn it all, where are those horses?"

"I do not know. Someone must have found them."

Behind them the pursuit had turned into a mob. Men, torches, guns—dozens of them. Justice stood with his arm around Toybo, grinding his teeth together. Bombo moaned in apprehension. If captured, they wouldn't be taken back to the adobe and locked up this time, not now. This time they would be shot, and unless Justice could think of a way to beat back that army with just two insignificant weapons, then that was exactly what was going to happen. He glanced at Toybo, saw the fear in her eyes, kissed her forehead once, and then stood waiting for their destiny.

14

Justice stood and watched until he could wait no longer. "Come on," he said to Bombo, "let's take it to them."

"Do what?" the giant asked in confusion.

"Give them a little taste of battle. See how they like being on the other end of the gun."

"They will cut us down, Justice," Bombo said.

"That," Ruff agreed, rubbing his chin, "is quite possible. But I'll not run anymore; I don't think I can. If you want to try it, give me the rifle."

"What about me?" Toybo asked.

"You?" Ruff kissed her again. "You are leaving, witch woman. Get! Head for the hills. I'll make sure they don't follow you."

"I am not leaving. I can help. I know where there are more bullets, more guns, many more guns."

Ruff turned slowly toward her, his eyebrow lifting. "You know *what*?"

"Where there are many more bullets. Maybe you can fight them off. There are more rifles too. One for me to fight with."

"Show me," Ruff demanded.

"*Ruff*, they are near now," Bombo said.

"Show me where the rifles are," Ruff commanded Toybo.

"Ruff Justice, they are crossing the wash. What can we do?" Bombo cried.

"What are you thinking?" Toybo asked.

"I'm thinking that we have an army. All we need is the weapons for them. If you know where there are guns . . ."

"What army?" Bombo wailed. "What are you talking about?"

"The slaves," Ruff replied.

"But the slaves are mostly women and children," Bombo said.

"It doesn't take a man to pull a trigger. Where are they, Toybo?"

"I saw them unloading many rifles from a wagon while I waited for a chance to free you. That woman, why was she so angry with you? What did you do to her?" Toybo wanted to know.

"Never mind that."

Bombo jabbed a thick finger toward the pursuers. "They are coming closer, Ruff Justice."

"What did you do with that woman, Ruff Justice? She was very beautiful and very angry."

"Toybo! Where are the weapons?"

"There is a small house. Across the valley, behind the big hacienda."

"Justice," Bombo said, "we cannot cross the valley."

"Guarded well?" Ruff asked.

"Three men," Toybo answered.

"Justice!" Bombo began to complain again, and Ruff turned on him.

"Give me your rifle. Give me your weapon and

walk over there. Let them knock you down and kick you and cut you and cart you off, half a man, to Chihuahua. You don't want to fight, then goddammit, get out of my way!"

Ruff reached for the rifle. But Bombo, half-angry, half-stunned, pulled it back. Turning his eyes down, he said, "Let us go. I will do what you tell me."

"Which way, Toybo?"

"This way, but please hurry, Ruff Justice. Please!"

They started through the trees again with the shouts from their hunters hurrying them on. Two wild shots flew through the trees overhead, but the vaqueros and the Apaches behind them couldn't have seen them. They were nervously fired shots, and cooler heads silenced the guns.

Ruff slowed his pace. The moon was only a faintly glowing memory on the horizon, but there was still too much light, too much to allow for a safe traverse of the valley. There were perhaps two hundred yards of empty field that had to be crossed. After that, they could weave among the trees and the outbuildings, but if they were discovered those first few hundred yards, there was no way at all to avoid being run down by the pursuing vaqueros.

Ruff breathed in slowly and looked to the others. Toybo nodded with urgency. Bombo shivered.

There was a brief moment when Ruff, poised for a dash across the field, stood bent forward, heart racing, feeling certain he had lost this last battle. Then Toybo touched his arm.

"Justice. There."

Looking to where she pointed, Ruff saw the dark, sinuous possibility.

They made the short dash to the gulley that was

washed into the earth and wound its way across the meadow toward the hacienda and the surrounding outbuildings. It was shoulder-high, and if they reached it and kept their heads down, they had a chance of making it.

Bombo let out a little moan as they ran for it, but they reached the gulley safely, leapt in, and started moving through it in a crouch, toward the hacienda. Toybo was at Ruff's shoulder.

"Which building?" he demanded.

"To the left. There is a lightning-shattered oak beside it. Two of the guards were in front, on a bench. Another was behind."

In five minutes they were near enough to see the building and, by peering slightly to the left, the guard at the rear. The other two men weren't visible. Maybe they had joined in the pursuit of the escaped prisoners. Ruff wasn't willing to take a chance on that guess now. He lay still, a softly breathing Toybo at his side, watching the hut.

He glanced to the sky. Was it graying in the east? He thought so. There wasn't going to be much time to put their haphazard plan into effect. They had to move now.

Ruff started up and then slid back, suddenly spotting the other guards. For some reason they had been on the far side of the building, perhaps talking to someone in the main house. Now they returned, yawning and chatting, to their bench. Ruff could hear their talk.

". . . some coffee."

"Why me? Why do you not go get it, Manuel?"

"If you do not get it, it will be gone. Then the breakfast mob will come in and we will get none at-all ..." The voices trailed off. The smaller man, grumbling and complaining, started toward the kitchen. He was the lucky one.

"Ruff?" Toybo touched his arm. "I will help."

"No." He tried to tug her back, but she was already gone, walking toward the dark hut. The vaquero swung his rifle around, saw that it was an unarmed woman, and lowered it again.

"Who are you? What do you want?"

"Nothing." Toybo had her hands behind her back. She swayed on her feet as she approached the guard, moving her hips rhythmically. "I was only lonesome."

"Lonesome, huh? Where did you come from, anyway? Who are you?"

Before Toybo could answer, the vaquero went down. Ruff Justice was a swiftly striking shadow. Crossing the empty space on silent feet, he hooked his forearm around the guard's neck and yanked back, clubbing him with his right hand simultaneously. The man went down.

"José?" a voice asked.

The man in the back called out softly, his voice expressing concern. He had heard the small sounds, the muffled groan. Justice looked at Toybo, then at Bombo, who was lumbering toward them. He snatched up the vaquero's big sombrero, picked up his rifle, and started around the building.

"José?" the voice repeated.

In the darkness the man backed away, his weapon wavering uncertainly. "Is that you, José?" he asked.

And then he backed right into the massive arms of Bombo, arms that clamped around him, squeezing the wind from him as his rifle was pinned uselessly to his side. When Bombo finally released the vaquero from the bear hug, the crushed man slumped to the earth and lay still.

"Come on. Quickly," Ruff ordered.

Toybo, her eyes flickering nervously, waited in front of the hut. Across the field she could see the torchlight, the weaving figures in the trees. They seemed close, too close.

"The door is locked," she cried to Ruff.

"Bombo?" he said, looking at the giant.

"I will try." The big Indian appraised the door for a moment, running his hand across it, before he braced himself and lunged. It didn't give the first time, but on the second try Bombo's impact carried him into the armory. From across the field, a cry of discovery went up.

Bombo, staggering back to the door, moaned again as he saw with certainty that the torches were coming nearer. Ruff brushed past him and filled his trouser pockets with .44-.40 cartridges. He found a gun belt and a spanking-new Colt and strapped it on.

"Ruff Justice?" Toybo said. There was fear in her voice, but the woman had character. She had seen a lot and had suffered much, and a few gunmen weren't going to start her weeping and complaining. "They are getting closer."

"Can you count them?"

"Ten—twelve."

Ruff was beside her, briefly draping a hand on her shoulder. "How good a shot are you?"

"With a bow and arrow or with a gun?"

Ruff smiled. "We have to use what we have." He handed her a Winchester repeater, fully loaded. She stared at him oddly for a moment, then nodded resolutely. She took the rifle and put it to her shoulder.

From inside the doorway they began firing. A dozen, two dozen shots in half a minute. The vaqueros, meeting the withering, unexpected fire, scattered in all directions, leaving dying torches on the field, leaving their comrades. A few hasty shots were fired in return, but they weren't even close.

Bombo had a gun in his hands, but he wasn't shooting. The big man was a gentle giant. He would rather let himself be hurt than hurt another living thing. Justice wished the world were filled with such men, but he knew it wasn't so, and what he needed now was an armed ally and not a philosopher of peace.

"Use that piece of iron," Ruff said sharply. "The bastards want to kill you, me, and the woman."

Bombo shook his head, fired three unenthusiastic shots, but failed to hit anything. Part of that was because the vaqueros had hidden themselves in every hollow and crevice they could find, behind every tree and rock, rick and outhouse.

"Let's go," Ruff said. "Bombo, gather up an armful of those Winchesters."

"Go where?" Toybo asked.

"To the slave quarters. Now, while Aguilar's men are disorganized."

"How many guns can he carry?" Toybo asked, nodding at Bombo.

"Plenty. A couple of dozen, why?"

"I know where there is a wagon. With horses hitched."

"You *what?*"

"At the barn we passed. You could not see it from this side, but I saw earlier last night. Maybe that is too far away."

"Maybe so, maybe not." Ruff looked that way. It still wasn't light. Maybe someone could cross that open space and find the wagon—if it were still there.

He made up his mind suddenly. "Try to cover me if they start firing."

"You are going for the wagon?"

"I am. If I don't get back—"

Toybo cut him off. "You *will* be back."

"Hope so. Cover me. Bombo?"

"All right. I will shoot them."

"Good man." Ruff smiled at Toybo and slipped out the door. There was no immediate fire and so he darted for the wash. As he leapt in, three or four guns opened up from various places on concealment. None of the shots was close. Bombo and Toybo shot back, but it would have been a wonder if their side scored any hits, either. It was still dark and damp. There was dew on the grass in the wash, diadems of dew hanging from the brush. The sun was on its way, though. The land was changing color, going red-violet in the distance as the highlands caught the first tentative rays of sunlight.

The barn was to Ruff's left. He came up out of the wash, running that way, rifle in hand, eyes searching the building. The wagon still stood there, loaded with lumber. The vaquero appeared above Ruff in the window of the hayloft. Justice shot him through the chest and he fell with a scream, his rifle clattering onto the bed of the wagon. The horses started, the off horse going up on hind legs, but Justice was already to the wagon box, already in control of the reins.

There wasn't time to unload the lumber, and so Justice just released the brake and whipped the team out of there, running them directly toward the armory, where occasionally he could see a puff of smoke as Toybo or the giant fired toward the trees across the meadow.

A bullet ripped into the dashboard of the wagon and Justice bent low, whipping the team on. The sun was yellow-orange in his eyes. Beyond the big house Justice could see men rushing toward the battle. Apaches. Sandfire hadn't taken all his people north, and now the Chiricahuas were coming to reinforce Aguilar's vaqueros. The fight was getting damned uneven.

Justice pulled up before the armory building in a storm of dust. The sun was brilliant through the trees and Aguilar's soldiers tried one fast, hard push at that moment. Justice leapt from the wagon box, rifle in hand, to stand behind the lumber wagon, firing rapidly into the ranks of the approaching vaqueros. One man dropped before his sights and then another, as enemy bullets splintered the wagon bed and panicked the horses, which tried their damnedest to pull against the hard-set brake.

Toybo was there with a newly loaded rifle, and Justice tossed his down. There was no shortage of ammunition now, nor of weapons. Time was all they were short on, and soldiers. Bombo was throwing rifles into the bed rapidly.

"Let's go," Ruff shouted as the vaqueros showed signs of weakening, pulling back. The Apaches were working through the trees now, and Ruff doubted they would retreat in the face of battle.

"Ruff . . ."

"Up, woman, we're going."

Bombo had a last armload of rifles, a last crate of

cartridges. He threw them aboard and then leapt into the bed after them as Justice whipped the horses forward, charging toward the hacienda, where half a dozen guns challenged them, before veering sharply away, toward the slave huts.

Toybo was shooting from behind the pile of lumber, emptying another of the dozen rifles she had loaded in advance. She wasn't hitting many of them, but two or three men did go down, and it had its effect: it slowed the pursuit considerably when they saw their comrades' blood staining the earth and suddenly realized that they too were mortal.

The slave huts were guarded by a small contingent of vaqueros. These had been watching the events across the field with interest and with humor. Now, as the battle swung toward them, charged down on them, their attitudes changed drastically, rapidly.

Guns were hastily and wildly fired by some; others made a dash for shelter, two men dropping their weapons as they ran.

They weren't all so hasty, though. One vaquero turned, dropped to his knee, and fired his rifle nearly into the face of Justice's wheel horse. Ruff gave the team the whip and the vaquero was trampled under, screaming horribly as the wagon crushed him into the earth.

The Apaches were coming now as Ruff reined in again in front of the slave quarters. Their war cries filled the air. Toybo and Bombo were still firing from the back of the wagon, but nothing seemed to slow down the pursuit as Sandfire's men charged on, firing and reloading, certain they had victory in their grasp. There was only the long-haired man, the dumb giant, and the woman.

Justice ran to the slave-quarters door and kicked at it, glancing over his shoulder as the Apaches rushed on, as the vaqueros reorganized themselves and advanced again. On the third kick the door opened and Justice went inside to see dark, frightened eyes, women clutching children to their breasts, babies crying.

"Do you want to fight or do you want to be slaves?" Ruff Justice demanded. The guns outside crackled loudly. The sun was bright gold, the interior of the slave quarters dark and musty.

"How can we fight?" a woman asked.

"Guns. I've got a wagonload of guns outside. Leave the young ones and take up a rifle. The Apaches are coming; this is your last chance. Fight or die."

15

They stared, just stared; then one woman of twenty or so, with a great bruise on the side of her face, stepped forward.

"Give me a gun," she said, "and I will fight them all."

"Good. Move now. Quickly!" Justice looked to the others. "Well?"

"They will kill us," a twelve-year-old boy said.

"That's right. If you don't take up a gun, you'll die—one way or the other. What are you, boy? Opata, I think. I have known Opata warriors before, brave men. What does a warrior do when the time comes to fight?"

"Give me a rifle," the boy said angrily.

Ruff felt bad about goading him into it, but there was nothing else to do. They were all dead if they didn't get enough fingers wrapped around those triggers.

Outside, the firing continued. "I must fight," Justice said. "Do what you want. Cower in here or help us fight your enemies, those who have killed your husbands and fathers, your brothers and uncles, those who would make slaves of you and your children."

Then, without waiting for a response, he turned on his heels and went out. There hadn't been time to wait for an answer. The Apaches were coming. Ruff wriggled beneath the wagon to lie beside the youth he had challenged into becoming a warrior. The kid scowled at Ruff, but Ruff only winked, snuggled up to the stock of his rifle, and fired off a round that caught a charging Chiricahua in the throat.

Something moved beside Ruff, and he saw one woman and then another, rifles in hands, resolute expressions on their dark faces, preparing themselves to fight the enemies of the mountains tribes, the Apache, and their allies, the soldiers of Don Carlos.

The guns roared from both sides now and the Aguilar men, who had been expecting easy pickings, went down or fell back hastily. There were also dead Apaches on the field, and the Indian slaves seemed to be bolstered by that, to believe for the first time that they could actually defeat their tribal enemies, the well-armed, bloodthirsty warriors led by Sandfire.

"Ammunition!" Ruff called without leaving his position.

Bombo distributed it, Bombo and a kid of seven or eight. They shoved a box of one hundred cartridges to Justice, and he jacked the lid off, smiling, as the Opata Indian woman next to him reached for a handful of brass shells to poke into the Winchester she was holding.

"I killed one man, maybe two," she said.

"We'll beat them," Ruff said.

But a minute later he wasn't so sure. The Apaches had a few tricks up their sleeves. They saw three ponies racing across the grass, their riders low behind the shoulders of the animals. Ruff watched them with narrowed eyes for a moment, puzzled. Then he saw what was up.

"Shoot them. Shoot those horses."

"What is . . . ?" And then everyone could see what was happening. The Apache riders were carrying torches, and from the shelter of their horses, they were setting the dry grass on fire. The wind was blowing directly toward the slave quarters and Ruff's war wagon. There was no escape behind them— Aguilar's men and the Chiricahuas would have already dispatched people to take up positions there. And when the fire hit the wagon, not only would flame and heat drive them out, but the cartridges it carried would go up like dynamite.

"Shoot the horses!" Ruff tagged one and it went down in a jumble, rolling over on his rider, who screamed out in pain and furry. But it didn't do a thing to stop the brushfire, which now, fanned by the morning breeze, was rushing toward them, crackling and roaring, dancing and curling, hungrily devouring all in its path.

"Ruff!" Toybo was beside him, anxious, frightened.

"Get into the slave quarters."

"We cannot—"

"We can't do anything else. The adobe won't burn. Do it! Take all the ammunition we can drag."

The Indian slaves looked suddenly dispirited, the heart taken out of them. There was something psychologically defeating about retreating to their slave quarters, their prison.

"Move it," Ruff urged them. "Come on—we'll stand them off from inside."

Now the Apaches were charging again, moving afoot in the wake of the fire. Ruff crawled from under the wagon and took the time to empty his Winchester in the direction of the Indians. The smoke was beginning to build, black and rolling, the flames orange against it.

"Get into the 'dobe," Ruff yelled again. Some of the slaves stood bewildered, guns dangling from their hands. Ruff snatched up one kid and carried him into the building where he took charge, commanding his Indian army.

"Knock those crates open. Four of you kids. You and you, hand out the ammunition. Woman, Opata woman! Get to this window. If you can't see, stand on an empty crate. Toybo! Some of these people don't speak English or Spanish. Translate, all right? And fast. Three people at the door. Take the table and chairs and make a barricade."

An Apache Indian showed his face at the window, and Ruff Justice, firing from the hip, shot him. A scream filled the slave quarters and the bloody mask vanished from the window.

"Hurry! You're supposed to be at that window! Get up there!"

It took a lot of prodding and repeating of commands—he didn't have an experienced cavalry platoon here—but he finally got them into position just as the fire reached them, licking at the adobe, sending smoke billowing in the windows, touching the wagon outside with tongues of flame.

The wagon went up in seconds. The explosion was deafening. Those near the door were hurled back as thousands of rounds of ammunition went up in a titanic blast that lifted the wagon and blew it to splinters. There were cries of pain on the heels of the explosion. Many Apaches, too near to the wagon, perhaps trying to get ammunition for their own guns, were killed by flying bullets as the hail of mindless lead was loosed by the fire. The adobe itself was peppered with bullets, but no one was hurt. The walls, meant to keep slaves in, luckily kept out the deadly missiles.

The smoke was dangerously thick. It filled the adobe briefly and Ruff thought they were going to lose a few people, but the wind, which had driven the flames across the field so rapidly, now pushed the smoke away from the adobe almost as quickly. The prisoners were able to rise from the floor, take their positions at the windows, and begin firing again as the onrushing Apache army charged the slave quarters.

The Apaches didn't have a chance. Rather, they had had a chance and they had muffed it. Now they were in the open, charging a fortified army. The fire had swept past to screen out their allies on the other side of the adobe.

The slaves cut them down as fast as they came. They fired until their rifle barrels were smoking and then they switched rifles, firing hundreds of additional rounds in minutes, pouring lead into the half-naked Chiricahua battle force.

And the Apaches retreated. A few of them. But that was all there was left: a few, a very few. Ruff Justice turned toward Toybo, his face smudged and grim.

"Let's get the rest of them."

The people were laughing, cheering, and leaping around; it was a minute before they realized Justice was talking to them.

"The Apaches are gone," they cried victoriously.

"Aguilar's people aren't. The slave masters. Palermo,

Alejandro, the others. They're forted up at the big house. What do we do about it?"

"Leave them alone. Let us go home."

"And you think Don Carlos will leave you alone when he gets back from the north? He'll come after you with vengeance and fire. He'll raid and kill and stamp out any resistance ruthlessly—he'll have to."

"What do we do, Ruff Justice? What can we do?"

"Destroy him. Destroy his men. Destroy this place. Burn the Rancho Paseo Prieto, burn everything in it and around it. Don't leave a memory of it standing! They wanted to fight with fire; very well, we can do it too. Let's not stop now and run. Let's finish the job we started!"

They weren't all buying that bag of goods, but that was all right. Justice didn't need them all, and he didn't want the weak, the nervous, or the cowardly. He didn't want the young ones and the old ones. He wanted a dozen good strong young women or youths, and he got them.

The volunteers stood by and watched while the others slipped out and made for the gully. Ruff had prepared his people to offer covering fire, but there were no shots from the hacienda. Justice waited until the others were well on their way and then turned to face the volunteers.

Bombo was there, head hanging. If he stood up straight, his head touched the roof of the slave quarters.

"Why don't you go too, Bombo? You've been plenty of help already."

"No," the big man replied. "I will stay, I will help, I will fight."

"We don't need you."

"Maybe not. I thought of what you said, though. I thought of others who might become slaves. Others who might be beaten, women who might be attacked. I will stay."

Ruff turned his eyes on Toybo, but she didn't even let him begin. "I am a fighter. Tell us what to do." Justice did, and in fifteen minutes they were moving out toward the hacienda, where a handful of Aguilar men were holed up.

For the first time Ruff's army had the advantage, and he knew it. They were going to torch that building, and after that was done, all they had to do was stand back and wait for the rats to emerge. And then it would be up to Aguilar's people—they could have it as they wanted it.

Surrender or die. Ruff hadn't decided what he would do with any prisoners they took. Maybe they could work out their lives as slaves to the mountain Indians.

Ruff and Toybo had worked their way across the burned field, through the scorched oak grove, to the wall of the hacienda. There had been no gunfire yet.

"Fire," Toybo said, "it is a terrible thing, a terrible weapon."

"Yes, it is," Ruff agreed. "But otherwise we're going to have to lose some women and some very young men to their guns. They've shown us what kind of people they are. They're willing to destroy us; we've got to be willing to fight for our own lives and for those of the others."

Toybo nodded and Ruff asked dryly, "Got a match?"

Not having seen but a handful in her life Toybo didn't, but she was a gem at starting a fire with steel and flint. She looked up worriedly at Ruff as she struck sparks; it still went against her nature to burn flesh, to injure wantonly. Ruff had to remind her.

"It's war, Toybo. It happens. We need to destroy the temple." He looked to the hacienda, built from the proceeds of crime and cruelty. "Those inside helped to build the temple."

She struck the flint again and crouched low to blow on the fire, to coax it to life. The sparks became tiny golden petals of flame and then a mushrooming crimson fire. Ruff and Toybo stepped back and watched the grass catch, watched the fire find new fuel and creep up the dry oaks, spreading from branch to branch and then leaping the hacienda wall with a menacing roar.

In minutes the whole world seemed to be afire: the trees, the shrubs in the courtyard of the hacienda, the walls surrounding it. Everything was dry in Sonora, and the fire became a raging beast.

"It's caught the house," Ruff said.

Toybo looked up. The eaves had caught and a trellis thick with vines went up as if it had been soaked in coal oil, flashing heat upward, seeming to strike new flames everywhere it touched.

Someone yelled and the guns started firing, though what good they were supposed to do was anyone's guess. But the windows of an upstairs room were broken out and the rifles blazed away.

A shout of triumph went up, audible even above the crash and thunder of the fires, as someone spotted Ruff Justice and rifles were trained on him. Ruff grabbed Toybo and they fell back into the fire-smudged oaks, bullets whining all around them. Ruff went to a knee and fired, and they saw a man cartwheel from a balcony, spin briefly through the air, and land in a fire-engulfed lath house.

A moment later they saw her.

Dolores Aguilar was on an upstairs balcony, her arms stretched out, head thrown back, and mouth open in a scream that didn't reach them. She wore a sheer white nightdress that did nothing to conceal her lush body. She screamed again and Justice growled a curse.

"What is it?" Toybo asked.

"What do you think? I have to get her."

"Her!" Toybo was wild with fury. "Why? What is she?"

"Just a woman."

"Beautiful," Toybo shot back. "You slept with her."

Ruff sucked in his breath sharply. He wasn't going to be drawn into that argument. "I can't leave her there to burn."

"You are leaving the others."

Yes, and Toybo knew the others were armed combatants, and Dolores was only a woman whose mind had been twisted by her life with her criminal family, who knew nothing of how people were to be treated except that they could be bought and sold, commanded—even to love you.

Looking into her deep, dark eyes, Ruff knew it would never be the same with Toybo if he went. Nor would he ever be the same man to himself if he didn't go up there.

"Try to cover me," Justice said, and then he was off, fighting his way through the flames toward the main gate. His arm across his face, he kicked at the iron gates until they collapsed inward. Ruff leapt them and rushed toward the house, a bullet from nowhere striking tile near his boot.

Then he was into the house. Flame was draped everywhere. The curtains were engulfed, the ceiling was crawling with fire. Dolores screamed and Ruff started up the stairs, through the corridor of hell.

He reached the landing and found the smoke heavier there, the heat more intense. Behind him a section of stairs collapsed with a roar.

Choking, eyes burning, Ruff worked his way down the upstairs corridor, trying to recall which was Dolores' room.

From a side door the flaming demon appeared. It was Palermo, his face blistered, smoke-darkened, his hair on fire.

"Bastard," he yelled, but Ruff's snap shot was first and Palermo was driven back into the inferno of the room behind him by a .44-.40 bullet that snuffed out Palermo's dirty little life.

The smoke was bad. Ruff ducked into a bedroom and whipped a blanket from a bed. There was a pitcher of water on a bureau across the room, above it a crucifix, large and expensively wrought. Ruff poured the water over the blanket and over his head, and went out again. He ducked low and ran up the hallway, where flames struck at him like fiery snakes.

Alejandro was there, but he was dead. Smoke had killed him, or flame, or a bullet from Ruff's army below. The smoke was around Justice like a deep fog now. He shouted.

"Dolores!"

He crouched, choking, waiting for an answer. But there was none, and he called out again and again.

"Dolores!"

"Help! Help me." The answer came at last, and Ruff went forward, the very floor beneath his feet burning now, sections of wall caving in, draperies flaring up brightly. The door before him was half-burned. Ruff kicked it open and went in.

"Dolores!"

She turned, lifted a finger, and started backing away, half-laughing, half-crying, cursing and shouting as she went.

"Filthy bastard! I could have made you happy. What was the matter with me? Why did you refuse me?"

Her nightgown was on fire and Ruff leapt forward to try to catch her, to smother the flames with his blanket, but she pulled away and leapt toward the balcony beyond the French window. Her hair was afire now too. Her nightdress went up like the wings of a moth. She turned a skull-like face to Ruff Justice, screamed something unintelligible, and then fell as the balcony, wrapped in curling flames, collapsed and carried her to her death.

Ruff rushed to the window, peered down at the burning corpse in the courtyard below, looked back at the wall of fire behind him, and then leapt through the empty space toward the huge oak tree below the window, as the great house of Aguilar collapsed, dying in flames, sending up sparks and smoke that could be seen for mile upon mile across Sonora.

16

Justice hit the oak tree hard. The wind was jarred from his lungs and the pain in his injured ribs flared up again. The flames around him played tag through the branches of the big tree.

He could see Dolores, still and blackened, but he couldn't see the wall, the gate, safety. The fire was everywhere, dominating the world. The heat was blistering his skin and singeing his hair. He climbed down, gasping for breath. He dropped to the earth from a low limb and staggered blindly forward, the flames urging him on.

He found Sagotal dead on the ground below the balcony. A short way on he found another vaquero. The Mexican had a neat round hole in the front of his head where a bullet had entered. There was no back to his skull.

Ruff moved on through the smoke and flames. Behind him a mammoth sound began to growl and creak and roll and grumble, and as he turned to look, the hacienda of Don Carlos caved in completely, sparks gouting high into the air, flames shooting out to all sides. Ruff smiled grimly, and then he thought of

Dolores lying there against the earth and the smile was washed away.

He was through the gate then, out into the cool, clean air, and Toybo found him, threw her arms around him, and held him briefly. "Justice."

"I'm all right."

"The woman . . . ?"

"Back there," he said, pointing to the carnage.

"Alive?"

"No, not alive," Justice said, and for just a moment there was a smile on Toybo's face, and it was an ugly thing to see. Justice clung to her for a while longer, but it wasn't the same, and when she drew away, he let her. It was over and they both knew it. The magic was gone.

"They are all dead," Toybo said.

"I think so, yes. The Apaches?"

"Gone. All gone."

"Good."

"Then we have won?" she asked.

"Very nearly." Ruff Justice looked to the rising sun and took in a deep breath. They had hardly begun, that was what he didn't want to tell Toybo, but she could read it in his eyes.

"What is it? What would you have us do?"

"Aguilar. McCoy. Sandfire. They're all still alive, they're all still hurting, destroying."

"You cannot be thinking of fighting them!"

"Of course. That's exactly what I'm thinking of, Toybo, you should know that."

"But it's impossible! You cannot expect these women, these *children*, to fight against Sandfire's best men."

"No. I can't expect that. They did well. I'm proud

of them all. As a matter of fact, it's more than that. I owe them all a debt of gratitude. I'd be dead, you would be dead, if they hadn't helped us."

"Then who . . . ?"

"Me." Ruff Justice looked at the woman, at the house which still burned furiously. "I'll finish them. I'll finish the job I started."

"You are crazy! You could not even find them."

"Sure I can. I know where they went."

"How could you?" Toybo asked.

"They went north. Do you know what day this is, Toybo?"

"What day?" She shook her head, the question had no meaning to her. "No."

"Well, I think I do. If I haven't lost track somewhere, it's the fifth of the month."

"I do not understand." She shrugged. "That means nothing, Ruff Justice."

"I think it does. When Dutch McCoy shot that officer at Bowie, he was being arrested for certain old crimes. But meanwhile, he was working on some new schemes—working with Aguilar, I think. Where had Aguilar been? In the north as well, across the border."

"I do not follow you."

"It's this way: Dutch McCoy had plans to hit the army payroll wagon on the fifth of the month. He and Aguilar. Some of Dutch's army cohorts talked and told Major Cavandish what was up. I don't see Aguilar giving up on the idea of taking an army payroll just because of a few snags. They've ridden north, all right, and taken an army with them. Whatever the cavalry is expecting, they're not expecting a band of Apaches and a private Mexican army to attack that payroll."

"It does not matter, Ruff Justice. You can do nothing about it now."

"Who says I can't?"

"They are miles ahead."

"Then I'll catch up. I'll try to beat them to Bowie and notify the army."

"You will never have that much time."

"I'll never know if I don't try. It's the only chance I have, unless . . ."

Toybo looked at him expectantly. "Yes?"

"Unless your brother and your people want to help me fight. Unless they want to strike back at the Apache for trying to push them from their land. They once said that they were brave men, as brave as the Chiricahua, but they needed weapons. Well"—Ruff nodded toward the captured Winchesters—"we've got weapons now."

"They will not do it," Toybo said.

"Why?"

"For you? For *me?*" Toybo asked bitterly.

"For themselves. Aguilar will be back if we don't stop him, and Sandfire. Aguilar will push your people out again, away from his slave route, his stronghold, where they might see or hear too much."

"I do not know . . ." She brightened. "But let us try it, Ruff Justice. The camp is on your way. We can cut miles off the trip, though, if we go through the dark canyon."

"Then let's go. Let's find us two fresh horses and get riding, Toybo."

Bombo was beside them again. He looked at Ruff and then at Toybo. "I do not want to fight anymore," he said.

"No." Justice put a hand on the vast shoulder of

the Indian. "Thanks for helping when you did, though. I won't forget you."

"No, and we will not forget you, Ruff Justice. Never. We will take guns and horses and go home."

Ruff found two good saddle horses, and a stocky sorrel to pack the rifles on. They worked swiftly, almost frantically.

By the time Ruff and Toybo were mounted, the slaves were heading out of the destroyed rancho toward the far hills. They lifted their eyes, raised hands, and waved to Justice; he waved back. He smiled briefly and then his face grew grim as he and Toybo raced across the long valley toward the Papago camp.

It was a long day. The horses were not fast enough, the sun was too swift to rise, the border was too far. By the time they entered the Papago camp, to be greeted by dark, suspicious faces, it was already nearly noon.

Thei and Iron Heart came together to meet Ruff Justice. Iron Heart scowled deeply. He hadn't forgotten their fight, not hardly. Thei wasn't much happier.

"What is this, Ruff Justice?" he demanded, and Ruff tugged at the rope that was wrapped around the blanket containing the rifles. The Winchesters fell free, clattering to the earth.

Thei sucked in his breath, crouched, and picked one up, putting his worn rifle musket away.

"What is this? Who are these for?" Toybo's brother asked.

"They're for you, Thei. And for Iron Heart. For all of your people."

"I do not understand," Thei said suspiciously. "Where did these come from? Why are you giving them to us? What is it you want of us, Ruff Justice?"

He told them.

Thei shook his head halfway through; he was still shaking it when Ruff finished. "We cannot do this."

"Why?"

"Against the Apaches—"

"It's *time*, Thei," Justice said.

"Time? I do not understand."

"Sure you do. It's time to find out what kind of man you are, to find out if the talking you do is just that, or if you are what you say you are, a man, a warrior, a leader."

"Are you saying I am not a warrior?" Thei stepped forward, the veins in his throat standing out as he clenched his jaw angrily.

"I'm not saying anything—except that it's time to find out who should be leading your tribe."

"Say the word," Iron Heart said savagely, "and I will kill this white."

Thei stretched out a restraining arm. He looked Ruff Justice in the eye, trying to read his motives, his thoughts. Was he simply goading Thei because he needed a Papago army? Or was he sincere, did he want to free the Papagos from fear of Sandfire? He had to decide one way or the other, and so he did.

"We ride with Justice. Fifteen minutes. Spread the word, hurry!"

Iron Heart hesitated briefly and then spun and ran off through the camp, summoning the warriors. Ruff was left with Thei and Toybo.

"I hope I am right in doing this," Thei said.

"You're right."

Thei then looked at Toybo. "The medicine. The medicine Aguilar gave my sister. It *was* bad, was it not, Ruff Justice?"

"It was bad. The Apaches wanted your land; Aguilar decided to give it to them."

"We drove her out," Thei said regretfully.

"Just remember that. There'll be another time in your life when you'll have to make another decision, Thei. Wisdom accumulates slowly. Toybo doesn't hold it against you."

"No, sister?" he asked Toybo.

"No, Thei."

They embraced briefly, and Ruff winked at Toybo over her brother's shoulder.

"But now I must prepare myself," Toybo said, breaking away.

"For what?" Thei asked.

"To travel with you, to the battle."

"You're not going," Justice said, and he looked at Thei, who nodded agreement.

"No, sister."

"But, Justice ..." She held his arm and looked into his eyes. He smiled softly, touching her hair with the back of his hand. Then she simply dropped his arm and walked away, leaving Justice and Thei alone.

"It's better," Ruff said. "Iron Heart still wants her. They're both Papago; they match a hell of a lot better than she and I ever would."

"I know this. I also know she wants you."

Ruff declined to answer. In minutes the Papago warriors gathered around them, Thei handing out new rifles to the more valiant and the better shots. Iron Heart was back, his face painted yellow and black. He rode a yellow horse.

"Let's ride, Thei," Justice said. "There's no time for war dancing."

"You know where Aguilar will attack the army payroll wagon?" he asked.

"I think so, I hope so. Twelve-mile Canyon. That's where I'd hit it, anyway."

"We may not get there in time to stop it."

"No, but we'll damn sure find them." He added resolutely, "And when we find them, they'll pay."

There wasn't time for more chatter, speech making, chest thumping. Ruff swung onto the back of the fresh pinto pony they had brought for him, and they rode out, Thei and Justice at the head of the Papago army. Only once did he turn back to see the small woman, the witch woman, watching from the deep shade of the spruce forest.

It was a long afternoon, over the hump, down the dark canyon, then out onto the flats, onto the raw, red desert. There was no conversation among the Papagos. No one spoke to Justice, and it suited him. He had his thoughts concentrated on only one thing: getting to where Aguilar and Sandfire and Dutch McCoy were, coming up on them unexpectedly with an army that must seem as if it had risen out of the sand to challenge them. They could have no inkling of what was happening behind them; the surprise would be total.

Ruff lifted his eyes toward the border, peering into the fierce glare off the desert. He wondered what he looked like at that moment. He still wore the torn and smudged suit Aguilar had given him, and the white shirt, which was nearer to black now, ripped wide open. His hair was singed; his face was unshaven. To top it off, he had tied a rag over his head for protection from the brutal Sonora sun, and that must have increased his piratical aspect. He was a fitting leader for a band of painted warriors, men with snakes and suns, scorpions and lightning depicted on their bodies, with bows and arrows, rifle muskets, or new repeating rifles in their hands, and the will to use them in their hearts.

"Where is this canyon, this Twelve-mile Canyon?" Thei asked.

"Ten miles."

Thei looked to the sun. "Are we too late?"

"I don't think so. The pay wagon always rolls in about dusk. We can make it. With luck."

Thei nodded. He lashed his pony with his quirt and leaned forward intently. He had made up his mind to fight and now he was eager to be at the canyon, to engage the Apaches.

Ruff was every bit as anxious to catch up with Aguilar, with his strutting son, with Dutch McCoy . . . and with Sandfire. He had been making himself silent vows all along the trail, vows to destroy the bastards, the murderers, the slavers. And he meant to keep the vows.

The horses ran on, pursuing time, while Ruff felt that it must be slipping away from them. The sun was sinking rapidly, and already there was color in the sky, color on the desert flats—deep purples, red violets, umbers, and soft violets.

"How far, Ruff Justice?" Thei asked again. "How far?" But Justice could only shake his head. The land didn't seem familiar. The peaks were in the wrong places; the shadows, deep and confusing, made a bewildering dark pool across the flats. They rode on.

Ruff was staring at the low hills, staring without thinking. His mind was dazed, blurred by travel and injury, by lack of food and proper rest. He just stared and then the knowledge of what he was staring at bloomed in his head like softly unfolding, brilliant fireworks.

"Twelve-mile," he said.

Thei turned to look at Ruff, who was pointing northward. "There it is," Justice said.

"Is there time, Ruff Justice? Is there time?"

"I don't know. I just don't know."

Could they be too late? Could Aguilar have hit the gold shipment, swung evasively north or east, leaving Sandfire and his people to separate and be swallowed up by the desert? Ruff hoped not. If there wasn't time to stop the robbery, he wanted there to be time at least to meet the Apaches and their Mexican commander head-on. Here and now.

He urged his horse forward. The little pinto was weary, but it had heart, and it lifted its pace at Ruff's insistence.

Suddenly they were into a fantastic deep gorge, painted purple by the dying sun, the ridges bright gold, serrated sharply.

"Did you see them?" Thei asked excitedly. "Did you see them, Ruff Justice?"

"See what?"

"Tracks. Many tracks. Fresh sign. Sandfire is ahead of us, and not far."

Now Justice picked up the tracks. The ground was hard, the shadows deep, but the tracks of the Apaches, of Aguilar's people, were evident.

The trail split with two golden tracks running off into the long canyon, one up to the highlands and one down toward the canyon bottom. Sandfire and Aguilar had gone down to the road that wound along the canyon floor. Thei looked to Justice.

"Which way?"

"Up. Let's take the high ground."

Iron Heart wanted to argue. "Sandfire is down below!"

"That's right. We want to be above him."

"I think you are running from him, Justice."

"Do you? Do you know what I think? I think one day you'll be a man, a warrior, a leader. On the day when you learn to control your emotions, Iron Heart, when you can let personal feelings out of decisions. We want the high ground to fight them. Thei?"

Justice looked to the Papago leader. He nodded. "We want the high ground. Justice is right."

They rode upward, moving slowly now, their horses' hooves whispering across the earth. The canyon was ablaze with crimson and red-violet, with gold and deep yellow-ocher. They crested the ridge and sat their horses while the cool wind washed over them at the hour of sunset. They could see the road winding away up the long canyon, could see a cloud of dust that had to be the army wagon and its payroll of gold.

And below them, among the rocks, they could see Aguilar and Sandfire.

17

Ruff Justice clambered down through the rocks, his rifle held high, his eyes alight with war fire. He knocked his knee against a boulder and stumbled, twisting an ankle, but he felt neither blow, not then.

His attention was on the road below them, only on the road. He crawled out on a large, sun-warmed flat rock, from which he had an excellent view of everything going on below. The payroll wagon, with its four outriders, was rolling toward them from out of the shadows to the east. Sandfire's people had taken up their positions in the yellow boulders below. Now they waited, silent and deadly as sidewinders. Aguilar's people were up a small feeder canyon, mounted, also waiting.

The attack couldn't fail. The soldiers were vastly outnumbered—or that's the way it must have seemed to Aguilar. Ruff could see the don, the silver on his sombrero and his saddle. Beside him was Ramón, haughty, cruel Ramón, and on the other side the red-bearded Dutch McCoy. They weren't going to risk their lives, put their bodies in the line of fire. Let the Apache dogs do their work.

Ruff turned as a scraping sound alerted him to Thei's approach. The Papago wriggled across the rock to lie beside Ruff.

"When?" Thei whispered.

Justice squinted into the canyon again. If they let the payroll wagon come too far, the soldiers would be killed. If they attacked too soon, before Thei's people were all in position, the Apaches might escape. The Papagos were working their way down through the canyon rocks now. Darkness was settling—that worried Ruff. The coach rumbled toward them. Everything was still in the canyon, although a hundred hearts were beating, a hundred minds preparing to fight, to kill, to die. A cottontail rabbit bounced away down a game trail.

Ruff Justice nodded and the guns opened up.

Justice saw it all at once: the smoke issuing from the barrels of the Papago rifles; the payroll wagon halting, being turned by the driver; the Apaches turning, answering the fire from above.

Seeing Aguilar break for the canyon, Ruff trained his sights on the animal's shoulder. And when he squeezed off, the horse went tumbling. Aguilar stayed down.

"Justice!"

At Thei's warning, Ruff looked behind him. Sandfire had had a few men above them—sentries, perhaps. If so, they had failed in their duty. One weirdly painted Apache, his body smeared with deer blood and mescal juice, leapt at Justice, war club raised high. Justice shot him through the chest and the Chiricahua fell beside him. Thei had taken the second attacking Apache, the bullet from his Winchester going through

176

the enemy Indian's body from side to side, tearing heart and lungs.

Justice saw him fall, but he had already returned his attention to the canyon below. They had the Apaches now, had them if they could close the trap. The rifle fire was staccato as the Papagos poured the ammunition through their rifles.

"Close in on them!" Ruff shouted above the racket. "We've got them cut off from their horses."

At a signal from Thei, the Papagos began to slip through the boulders as the Apaches pulled back into a tighter knot. Those who tried to break out were shot down from the rocks above.

"Justice!" Thei touched his shoulder and jabbed a finger up the canyon. Two men were riding pell-mell away from the fight. Ruff Justice cursed, shoving fresh loads into his rifle. He had taken his eyes off them for a moment, and now Ramón and Dutch McCoy had made their break.

"Finish it off, Thei," Justice said. "You've got the Apaches cooked."

"You are going after them?" Thei asked.

Justice looked toward the two fleeing horsemen. "What do you think?" He started up through the rocks toward his pinto pony.

Dutch and Ramón had a good lead on him, but they were going to have to ride either past or over the army patrol to get out of Twelve-mile Canyon. Ruff thought he had them.

In no time, he was onto the pinto and down the trail, glancing anxiously toward the skies. It was growing dark fast. The guns behind him continued to fire repetitively, but the battle was slowing. The Apaches were being squeezed hard. It was all over for

177

Sandfire, whether or not he got out of this alive. His army would be broken, defeated.

Ruff wound down a narrow trail and hit the floor of the canyon, riding fast. The little pinto reached its stride quickly, Justice bending low across the withers, eyes straining into the dusk, wanting to find targets for his guns.

Then, from ahead, the rifle fire sounded and Ruff Justice smiled. It was a dark smile, humorless. They had run into the army patrol, and they were finding out what soldiers thought of people who wanted to take their pay from them.

Ruff slowed the pinto a little. The bottom of the canyon was sand and shadow. Strange, misshapen boulders rose up beside the trail. The guns behind him had blended with the silence, and those ahead had sputtered briefly and fallen silent. All around him the war was ending.

Justice saw the dark figure of a lathered horse charging toward him, and he managed to hurl himself from the pinto's back just as Dutch McCoy, firing from horseback, tried to put a bullet through his heart.

McCoy looked haunted. Blood trickled from his mouth. His cruel, savage little world was falling apart.

"Justice!" he shouted, reining in his horse with a vicious yank.

It was the last thing Dutch McCoy ever said. Justice hit the ground, rifle in hand, and from a kneeling position he pumped three rounds through McCoy's thick body, slamming him from his horse's back to the ground. He lay still, his fingers twitching uselessly around the butt of the pearl-handled revolver he carried. Ruff kicked the gun away and stood over

McCoy, watching him die as the sun set, and when it was over, he walked away, feeling no remorse whatever.

The little pinto was trembling when Justice found him and swung onto its back to ride more slowly up the trail. He found the remains of Ramón Aguilar a short distance on. Three soldiers were around the body. They turned at the sound of the pinto's approaching hoofbeats, and Justice raised his hands and called out, "We're on the same side, boys!"

"Yeah. Who says? Who the hell are you?"

"Ruffin T. Justice, civilian scout out of Fort Bowie."

"The *hell* it is," one of the soldiers said in amazement, and he walked nearer to Justice, peering up at him. "Why, hello, Mister Justice. Corporal Taggart—remember me?"

"Sure do, Tag. How's things?"

"All right now, I guess."

"Mind if I put my hands down?" Ruff asked.

"No, of course not. Say, what's going on up ahead? We were trying to decide whether to fort up or hightail it out of here when these two came charging at us. Dutch McCoy I damn sure knew, and he started firing. So did the Mex. Who was he?"

"Just another cheap crook," Ruff told them.

A second soldier, one Ruff didn't know, asked, "What's going on ahead? Can we go through?"

"You'd be better off driving around. It won't cost you a lot of time."

"What was happening anyway?"

"Indians. You know how Indians are. Trying to kill each other off," Ruff said. He was too tired physically and mentally to explain it all. They were looking at him oddly, he realized, but it didn't matter.

He knew how he looked, like a guest at a fancy-dress ball who had gotten enormously drunk and then been run over by a locomotive and sixteen cars.

"You want to ride on the wagon, Mister Justice?" Taggart asked with some concern. He *did* look as bad as he felt, Ruff thought.

"No," Ruff said. "I'll go in alone."

He felt suddenly drained, empty, satisfied with himself. The purple dusk was pleasant; the breeze that sang in the canyon and moved his long dark hair was cooling; the war was ended. Bowie lay ahead. Was there time to wash and dress and escort Alicia to her Uncle Fernando's cantina? How long had it been since he had seen that big, enthusiastic woman?

For a moment he stood there, thinking of Alicia and then of a witch woman who lived to the south, a good woman, a leader for her people.

"You all right, Mister Justice?"

"Me? Hell, yes. Next time you see me, Tag, you touch me for a drink, all right? You boys better get riding. If I know the cavalry, there's a lot of men waiting to hear the pay wagon roll in."

The wagon pulled out, Taggart lifting a hand to Justice. There was still a crimson smear against the western sky, but it was as near to dark as it could get. Justice watched the night arrive.

He considered going back to see how Thei and Iron Heart had fared, but that seemed like intruding. They had won their battle against the Apache; they didn't need him hanging around.

He took the pinto's reins, looked once at the twisted body of Ramón Aguilar, and started out of Twelve-mile. He began to sing.

180

> Everyone knew that red-head lady
> That belle of the ballroom, our three-legged
> Sadie . . .

He leapt at Ruff from the rocks, and Justice saw the knife in Sandfire's hand slash toward his throat. Ruff kicked free of the stirrups and threw himself to one side, landing hard as the Apache war leader hit the paint pony and rolled aside. The little horse panicked. Sandfire hit the ground just as Justice came to his feet, rifle in hand. The Apache lunged at Justice, and when the Winchester detonated, the bullet caught him flush in the face. Sandfire collapsed against the sandy floor of the canyon to lie there in a pool of his own slowly leaking, warm blood. Ruff Justice shook his head.

"Music critics," he muttered. Then he collected the reins to the little paint and started northward again, singing his way home to where Alicia waited.

WESTWARD HO!

The following is the opening chapter from the next novel in the gun-blazing, action-packed new Ruff Justice series from Signet!

RUFF JUSTICE #21: THE DENVER DUCHESS

1

The tall man, dressed in buckskins, stepped from the railroad car onto the station platform. He had a satchel in one hand and a .56-caliber Spencer repeating rifle in the other. He took in slow, deep breaths of the cool, clean air. The sign on the depot eaves read: DENVER, COLORADO ALT. 5,280 FT.

Lifting his eyes, the tall man could see the peaks of the high mountains, the Rockies, stretching their grandeur skyward. Massive and sprawling, they were beautiful, raw, and just a little intimidating.

"Ruffin!" a voice called out.

The tall man turned his head toward the voice, which belonged to a reedy blond man in a sheepskin coat. There was a badge pinned to his blue flannel shirt.

Ruff Justice put down his bag and rifle and stuck out a hand, which the other man took warmly.

"How's everything, Les?"

"Fine, Ruffin. Just fine." He still held Ruff's hand. The two men stood looking at each other, assuring themselves that an old friend still walked the earth despite the hazards of life. "I couldn't believe it when I got your wire. I would have thought you were buzzard bait long ago."

"They keep trying," Justice answered with a smile. "Still town marshal, I see. They haven't squeezed you out yet."

Les Coyle smiled thinly. "They keep trying, Ruff. They keep trying." Then he slapped Justice on the shoulder and said, "Come on uptown. We can walk. You want to stay at the jailhouse or are you flush enough for the Grand Hotel?"

"The army still pays me," Justice told Coyle. "I'll try the Grand again. They still got running water or did that experiment bust?"

"They've got it," the marshal said. "The damn holding tank busted last winter, sheeted the front of the hotel with ice, but they've got it all back together now. I hear the place across the street is going to try it as well. Next thing you know there'll be running water everywhere."

Denver hadn't changed, and yet it was greatly different, Justice thought. It still bustled, hustled, built up and tore down; you could still see drunks and whores on the streets at nine in the morning, find a cutthroat to do a quick midnight job for you, lose a fortune at faro or win a year's wages on the spin of a wheel; the gold mines were still turning out enormous profits for the lucky few, becoming slave pits for the many, and financial heartbreakers for some. Denver was still the richest city between the Mississippi and San Francisco. The overnighters, the miners who found themselves sitting on top of a mountain of gold ore and hadn't an idea in the world of how to spend it, were still building their mansions on the outskirts of town, touring Europe to loot it of art objects and its veneer of culture, and coming home even richer and only a little wiser.

Yet it had changed. The old Amory House had been burned down by an arsonist angry at the loss of his stake in a poker game. Wichita Charley, who used to roam the streets in a bearskin and ten-gallon hat— winter or summer—had been killed by an unknown person with no sense of humor or tolerance. They had paved a section of Central Avenue with red bricks; Hadley's tent-town mercantile had gone from canvas to frame and clapboard. There were a hell of a lot more people.

"I've got seven deputies," Les Coyle told Justice, "and that's not half enough. If you ever want a job wearing a badge . . ."

"No, thank you! I've got enough trouble in my life," Ruff said with a smile.

"I hear you look for half of it."

"Maybe. It kind of careens toward me, though."

"Ruff . . ." Les Coyle stopped, smiled boyishly, and scratched his arm. "I'm gettin' married."

"Well, damn me. You don't mean it."

"I do," Coyle said hastily. Then he grew meditative. "You don't think . . . I'm a lawman, Ruff . . Some folks say it's wrong for a lawman to marry and have kids. You know how it gets in these towns when the midnight fever strikes. Every man on the street's got a gun, and every other one wants to plug me for one reason or the other."

"You're asking me what to do?" Ruff laughed. "Hell

Les, you must want her. She must want you. She knows what you do for a living. Don't let other people do your thinking for you. You two know what's best."

"Yeah. It's just—"

"It'll hurt her as much, maybe more, if you were never man and wife—if and when it happens. Christ, look at you. You must be old enough to go on pension now anyway! You can't have many working years left."

"I'm a year older than you, Ruffin T. Justice, and you know it. Those are worry lines on my face, something you wouldn't know about."

They started up Bond Street, crossed the road at the Cassio Brothers Store, climbed the steps, and entered the marshal's office, which was situated above the store.

Ruff looked around, nodded, put his bag down, and tossed his hat on the desk. "Home?" he asked.

"For now. We've got a little place outside of town— back near Colson Canyon. Lily's still fixing it up." Coyle hung his head sheepishly. "You know, yellow curtains and such."

Ruff had been reading the wanted posters on the wall. Now he plopped himself into Les Coyle's swivel chair.

"When do I get to meet her?"

"Tonight. If you want to. I didn't—"

"Come on, Les. What do you think I want to do? Of course I want to meet her. Give you my approval and all."

"Maybe I'm afraid to let you near her," Coyle joked.

"Maybe you should be. Tonight?"

"Sure . . . Well, why don't you go with us?" the marshal said, brightening.

"Go with you where?" Ruff asked.

"To the ball. All of Denver's going. I even got an invite. Not because of me, but because Lily knows all those folks, you see. Her mother was some kind of cousin removed."

"Les, you know I have no idea what you're talking about, don't you? As for any kind of ball, what I had in mind was a peaceful night at the Grand—a hot bath, a meal, a soft pillow." All of which would be a great change from sleeping out on the Mexican desert, living off roots and dried venison, which was what Justice had been doing for the past few weeks before stepping on that northbound train and heading for Dakota. He had decided to spend a few days in Denver to get warm and spoiled and to look up a few old friends like Les Coyle. He was ready for some of that warmth and spoiling now. Not for some fancy-dress ball.

"The Duchess is staging this thing, Ruff. In a way it's kind of an engagement party for me and Lily. Duchess Duchamp-Villon." Coyle chuckled. "The former Katie Price."

"Didn't she work at the Scottish Wheel?"

"The same. But she didn't *work* there, Ruff, she owned it. Yes, our Katie was something even then, beautiful and well-off, huh? But when this Duke Duchamp-Villon came over here to buy the Never-Never Mine from Willy McDowell and the Ute—"

"They sold out?" Ruff interrupted, surprised at the news.

"Yes, just before the Never-Never opened up onto

a vein six yards wide of jewelers'-grade gold. Well, McDowell got so mad he drank himself to death. The Ute spent all of his take on cloth and beads and trade knives and then went back to the mountains to live like a king among his own people."

"And the Frenchman got wealthy?"

"Well, he already was, you see. He worked for some sort of cartel, but he had a stake in it too. Yes, he got rich. And then he got lonely, and then he got Katie Price out of the Scottish Wheel, and then he got killed."

"Here?"

"Right here. After he and Katie got back from a six-month honeymoon in Europe. Now the Duchess is *very* rich. She's got a three-story stone house on Gower, with gold fixtures in the bathrooms—twelve of them! And you think the men around here don't chase her? Good Lord! But she's not high-toned around folks, Ruffin. She knows that, underneath, she's still Katie Price. So she gives a costume ball like this, and she invites all her old friends as well as the upper crust."

"A costume ball. Now I know I'm not going."

"Not even to meet Lily?"

"No."

"Or for a chance to see our Denver Duchess up close?"

"No."

"Not for anything in the world, even though I've got a costume made up for you and everything?" a soft female voice asked.

The second voice came from behind Justice. It was

pearly and gentle as velvet, inviting and feminine, and Ruff turned slowly to its summons.

"Please?"

She was tall, her dark hair stacked and curled beneath a tiny hat. Her figure was lush and undeniable beneath the black silk that was draped lovingly over her body. Her lips were full; her nose softly arched, nostrils flaring; and when she smiled, she revealed even white teeth. Her green eyes sparkled with the invitation that the tilt and thrust of her hips seemed to imply.

"I'm not used to being refused," the Duchess Duchamp-Villon said to Ruff Justice. "I'd like you to come to the ball. I'm in mourning, but I could offer you a dance."

It seemed she was offering much more than that. Justice glanced at Les, and damn him, he was smiling. The marshal knew that Justice wasn't the kind to turn down an invitation like this one. And he was dead right.

"Tonight, then," Justice said, bowing from the neck.

"Tonight," the Duchess of Denver said. "Yes, I believe it will be tonight."

Exciting Westerns by Jon Sharpe from SIGNET

(0451)

- [ ] THE TRAILSMAN #1: SEVEN WAGONS WEST   (127293—$2.50)*
- [ ] THE TRAILSMAN #2: THE HANGING TRAIL   (110536—$2.25)
- [ ] THE TRAILSMAN #3: MOUNTAIN MAN KILL   (121007—$2.50)*
- [ ] THE TRAILSMAN #4: THE SUNDOWN SEARCHERS   (122003—$2.50)*
- [ ] THE TRAILSMAN #5: THE RIVER RAIDERS   (127188—$2.50)*
- [ ] THE TRAILSMAN #6: DAKOTA WILD   (119886—$2.50)*
- [ ] THE TRAILSMAN #7: WOLF COUNTRY   (123697—$2.50)
- [ ] THE TRAILSMAN #8: SIX-GUN DRIVE   (121724—$2.50)*
- [ ] THE TRAILSMAN #9: DEAD MAN'S SADDLE   (126629—$2.50)*
- [ ] THE TRAILSMAN #10: SLAVE HUNTER   (114655—$2.25)
- [ ] THE TRAILSMAN #11: MONTANA MAIDEN   (116321—$2.25)
- [ ] THE TRAILSMAN #12: CONDOR PASS   (118375—$2.50)*
- [ ] THE TRAILSMAN #13: BLOOD CHASE   (119274—$2.50)*
- [ ] THE TRAILSMAN #14: ARROWHEAD TERRITORY   (120809—$2.50)*
- [ ] THE TRAILSMAN #15: THE STALKING HORSE   (121430—$2.50)*
- [ ] THE TRAILSMAN #16: SAVAGE SHOWDOWN   (122496—$2.50)*
- [ ] THE TRAILSMAN #17: RIDE THE WILD SHADOW   (122801—$2.50)*
- [ ] THE TRAILSMAN #18: CRY THE CHEYENNE   (123433—$2.50)*
- [ ] THE TRAILSMAN #19: SPOON RIVER STUD   (123875—$2.50)*
- [ ] THE TRAILSMAN #20: THE JUDAS KILLER   (124545—$2.50)*

*Price is $2.95 in Canada

Buy them at your local bookstore or use this convenient coupon for ordering.

NEW AMERICAN LIBRARY,
P.O. Box 999, Bergenfield, New Jersey 07621

Please send me the books I have checked above. I am enclosing $_____
(please add $1.00 to this order to cover postage and handling). Send check
or money order—no cash or C.O.D.'s. Prices and numbers are subject to change
without notice.

Name _____

Address_____

City_____State_____Zip Code_____

Allow 4-6 weeks for delivery.
This offer is subject to withdrawal without notice.

Exciting Westerns by Jon Sharpe

**Buy them at your local
bookstore or use coupon
on next page for ordering.**

SIGNET Westerns You'll Enjoy by Leo P. Kelley

JOIN THE *RUFF JUSTICE* READERS' PANEL

Help us bring you more of the books you like by filling out this survey and mailing it in today.

1. Book Title: _____

   Book #: _____

2. Using the scale below, how would you rate this book on the following features? Please write in one rating from 0-10 for each feature in the spaces provided.

	NOT SO				EXCEL-
POOR	GOOD	O.K.	GOOD	LENT
0 1	2 3	4 5 6	7 8	9 10

RATING

Overall opinion of book .... _____
Plot/Story .... _____
Setting/Location .... _____
Writing Style .... _____
Character Development .... _____
Conclusion/Ending .... _____
Scene on Front Cover .... _____

3. About how many western books do you buy for yourself each month? _____

4. How would you classify yourself as a reader of westerns? I am a ( ) light ( ) medium ( ) heavy reader.

5. What is your education?
   ( ) High School (or less) ( ) 4 yrs. college
   ( ) 2 yrs. college ( ) Post Graduate

6. Age _____   7. Sex: ( ) Male ( ) Female

Please Print Name_____

Address_____

City _____ State _____ Zip _____

Phone # (_____)_____

Thank you. Please send to New American Library, Research Dept., 1633 Broadway, New York, NY 10019.